THE HOUSE ON THE MOOR

A Haunted House book

William Meikle

DARK RENAISSANCE BOOKS
2015

FIRST TRADE PAPERBACK EDITION

Editor & Publisher, Joe Morey

ISBN: 978-1-937128-70-8

Interior design by F. J. Bergmann

A Haunted House book

Dark Renaissance Books
Brookings, OR 97415
www.darkrenaissance.com

List of Illustrations

For Alan Garner, Oliver Postgate and Robert Louis Stevenson,
who lit the flame.

1

"Tell me again: what are we doing here?"

John noticed, too late, that Carole was in that fed-up state that was perilously close to heading into a full-blown shouting match. He patted the side of the too-soft bed and invited her over to sit beside him. She walked across the room—reluctantly, but she did it—sitting down so as to leave a two-foot gap between them, as if inviting him to try and cross it. He tried not to rise to the bait.

"I told you. I need to do an interview—and this one's important to me. It's not just another job," John replied. "Besides, it's a nice long weekend for you. I'll be working, but it shouldn't take me long though—he's an old man, and I've been told he's only good for an hour or so in the morning before the lights go dim and he needs to rest up. Then we'll have most of each day to ourselves to explore."

Carole motioned to the window, where sheets of rain lashed against the glass in patterns that were almost rhythmic.

"You've brought us to the wilds of Scotland—in March. How much exploring do you expect to get done? You saw what we passed on the way here—bog, cows and hills, and not a Starbucks in sight. I'd have been better off staying at home—at least that way I might have got a decent cup of coffee."

On that point, John would happily have agreed with her, if

he thought it wouldn't lead to an argument. When he'd found out about the job the week before, he'd considered coming on his own, but there had been a recent tiff about him leaving her alone on too many weekends, so he'd invited Carole on this one. He'd told her they were going to Scotland—what he hadn't said was that it was twenty miles from anywhere, in a drafty mansion on a patch of remote moorland, with only an old retired man and two equally old servants for company. That—and the inclement weather that looked like it had set in for the duration—meant that their long weekend wasn't getting off to the best of starts.

He'd known as soon as the taxi crested a hill and they got their first look at the property that he was in for some trouble. The trip north from Inverness Airport had cost fifty quid, it had taken over an hour, and, by the time they drove up onto the high moor and had a look down the long driveway to their destination, Carole had already got her not-best-pleased face on. It didn't help that it had been raining since they got off the plane, constant heavy drizzle that washed everything to misty gray.

The house itself was in the old Scots style—gray granite and little more than a squat ugly block with little in the way of adornment or finery. It had obviously been built for function in a spot where few people were ever going to see it to appreciate anything more aesthetically pleasing. Long-dead branches of crawling ivy dotted with a few yellow leaves stubbornly clinging on against the weather ran across the walls like dried-up veins. The windows appeared to contain original leaded glass, black, like unblinking eyes watching their approach all the way down the drive. The thick slates on the roof were green with mossy slime and looked as old as the hills from which they had been cut.

There were no formal gardens here, no trimmed box hedges or fine mazes, just stunted clumps of gorse and heather interspersed with dark stagnant pools of slow-developing peat on either side of the pothole ridden gravel track. A fine mist defied the drizzle and hung in patches, drifting back and forth across the moor.

Behind the house itself, some ten miles distant across a longer expanse of bog, was a range of cloud-shrouded hills. In the dim light they looked black, almost menacing. Apart from a marching row of telegraph poles that headed off in that direction, there was no other sign of life to be seen in the whole panorama.

The taxi let them off at the door and drove off in a spray of gravel in the driver's hurry to depart.

An aged butler was already waiting to show them inside, through an echoing hallway that smelled slightly musty and damp, and up a long ornate staircase to the room where they currently sat on the edge of the bed, on the verge of yet another argument.

"Look, Carole," he said. "I don't want a fight."

"Then don't talk to me," she replied.

She stood and started to unpack, throwing clothes willy-nilly into the small chest of drawers under the window. Her back was ramrod-straight, daring him to speak. He knew all the signs—an explosion was only seconds away.

He was saved by a knock on the door and opened it to see the old butler in the hallway.

"The Maister will see you whenever you are ready, sir. He has asked that you see him alone. The lady may take tea in the front sitting room, where there are some fancies laid out on the table."

"Fancies!" Carole mouthed, and smiled for the first time since getting off the plane in Inverness.

John's mood was slowly starting to improve as he followed the old butler downstairs.

His improved mood meant that he actually paid attention to the house on his way down the staircase, which was wide and handsome, with a polished mahogany banister and elegant, thick-pile carpeting. If the exterior of the house had looked rather drab and uninspiring, the interior more than made up for any lack of opulence. The walls were festooned with portraits, landscapes, and the heads of dead animals, obviously a legacy of a long history of hunting in these parts. The hallway at the foot of the stairs had no carpets, but a stunning mosaic floor depicting yet another hunting scene, with a magnificent stag being run down by hounds on a highland mountainside.

And the best was yet to come.

The butler showed him into a high-vaulted library that rose through an interior column the full height of the house. There were three floors of it, ancient oak shelves crammed tight with leather-bound books, some dusty and unloved, others obviously well read and cared for. Balconies ran the full circumference of each floor, connected by ornate wrought iron staircases between levels. John was momentarily dazzled by his sheer delight in the place—he would happily spend several months among these shelves.

He was brought back to reality by a discreet cough from the butler at his side.

The man he had come more than five hundred miles to interview was sitting in a large wing-backed armchair, as close to a roaring fire as he could get without being burned. His legs were covered by two thick tartan throws, but John guessed they would be as thin as the rest of him. His hands looked too large on wrists that might snap at any moment. His head, bald, liver-spotted and partially tucked inside a heavy woolen pullover, made him look more like a slightly startled turtle than a man who had been a famous philanderer and roué in his day—a day that was long since past.

"Mr. Fraser, I presume?" the old man said, and cackled until he was forced to stop when it brought on a coughing fit.

John nodded, and considered putting out a hand to be shaken, then thought better of it—the old man didn't look to be up to the effort.

"Pleased to meet you, Mr. Blacklaw," he said. The old man managed to lift a hand enough to wave John to the seat opposite his across the fireplace. John moved the heavy chair away from the direct heat before sitting down.

John had expected an exchange of pleasantries, perhaps an introduction, but Blacklaw got straight to the point.

"You look just like him," the old man said. "I was prepared to answer your questions—but I wasn't prepared for that."

"My mother always said I had his eyes," John said, more for something to say than from any real idea where to push the conversation.

"Oh, it's more than that," Blacklaw said. "You're almost his double. He affected a full beard, but that wasn't unusual back then. And apart from that, you even have his build—and his walk. I can see why he interests you."

And the old man across the fireplace held the key to the last chapter …

John hadn't spoken to the old man when setting up the interview—he'd spoken to a woman—the housekeeper, he'd guessed, and the rest of the deal had been conducted by letter—word-processed and printed from John, hand-written in a crisp, clear hand from the old man's end. All the correspondence was in aid of one goal—John was researching a book, a biography of his grandfather.

And the old man across the fireplace held the key to the last chapter—if only John could get him to talk about it.

2

Carole made her way downstairs five minutes after John, taking her time to study the paintings and trying her best to ignore the stares of the dead animals as she descended. There was only one door open—at the front of the house near the main entrance. She walked into a large room, the focal point of which was a long mahogany dining table. It was handsome, though battered, capable of seating twelve, and of a quality that would make a London antique dealer drool with anticipation of a hefty commission.

A high bay window to the front looked out over the moor, but Carole ignored that and went straight to a long buffet table against the wall where several trays of cakes and small, sweet treats had been laid out. She resisted the urge to take one of everything and put half a dozen of them—the ones that looked least likely to go straight to her hips—on a plate before taking it and a chair over to the fireplace..

She heard the men speaking next door, but only as a low drone—she was unable to make out any words, and it sounded like the old man they'd come to see was doing most of the talking. She pulled her chair closer to a two-bar electric fire dwarfed by a huge stone grate, and picked up her first of what would prove to be many sweets.

The "fancies"—clearly homemade, and fresh that very morning—proved to be the highlight of the trip so far—

although Carole foresaw a sugar high in her near future that would mean a crash at some point later. She stared out at the moor and tried not to think about the long weekend ahead that was going to feel like an eternity.

Rain washed in sheets down the window, softening and blurring the landscape outside and making it look like the early stages of an amateur watercolor painting, the view punctuated with infrequent glimpses of a water-soaked driveway surrounded by featureless moorland. Once she saw someone walking in the distance, a squat figure huddled against the elements, tramping through the bog with what looked like grim determination. For an instant Carole was actually glad she was inside, in the dry—then a cold breeze blew through the ground floor, as if someone somewhere had opened a door, and she was forced to huddle closer to the fire.

She had another fancy, but she was close to making herself sick with them—this one tasted cloying, over-sugared and too heavy on the marzipan. She only managed one bite, then put the plate down on the floor at her feet. The butler was at her side in seconds to remove it. Carole tried to make conversation, but the man was all business, calling her "ma'am" and making her feel like an elderly invalid herself. She let him shuffle off and went back to staring out the window.

I should have let him come on his own.

It wasn't the first time she'd had the thought, and wouldn't be the last. She had indeed been pissed off at him for leaving her alone at weekends when his research called him away—

so pissed off that she'd more or less demanded to come along on this trip. She'd hoped for Edinburgh, shops, good hotels and restaurants—anything but this dreary, damp monstrosity on the edge of nowhere.

What the hell am I going to do here all weekend?

The rain got heavier, concealing the view even further, and the light was going now as the afternoon progressed. In the gloom she saw that the hunched figure she'd noticed earlier was back, going in the other direction now, but still bent over, as if battling a wind although the drizzle was falling almost straight down. She felt cold again, and resolved to wear thicker clothing for the duration.

It's not as if we're going to be going out anywhere.

She almost jumped when the butler appeared at her shoulder—she hadn't heard him, almost as if he had glided in on castors. She smiled at that thought, then saw the puzzled expression on the old man's face, and she blushed, afraid he might think she was laughing at him.

"I'm sorry—you startled me," she said, but once again the man was all business and efficiency.

"Dinner will be served at eight if ma'am needs time to prepare," he said. If she'd had the energy, she might have taken that as a slight on her appearance, but there seemed to be no guile or malice in the old man's smile as she nodded in reply. Once he had left the room she rose and followed him out to the hallway.

The chilly draft was even more pronounced here, coming from somewhere at the rear of the house, and from where she stood she could now hear the familiar clang and rattle of pans and crockery as food was prepared. To her right the door to the library was now partially open and she caught a glimpse of John at the fireplace—head tilted slightly to one side as he always did when he was listening intently. It did not look like he was going to be finished anytime soon.

She considered interrupting the conversation, but she was a guest here, and manners and protocol were clearly of some importance—although that wasn't anything that normally bothered her. But John looked so serious—and she was too tired for an argument right now. The journey to get here had taken more out her than she'd realized. It had been an early start, followed by delays at the southern end, and a cramped flight full of crying babies, noisy teenagers and bad food. Add in the long dull taxi journey, and a nap before dinner sounded like just the thing to recharge her batteries.

She went back upstairs to their room, trying again to avoid the stares from both the ancestral portraits and the heads of deer, foxes and boar that watched her all the way up. She flopped on the bed and checked her watch—it was just after four in the afternoon.

"Plenty of time," she muttered.

A minute later she was fast asleep.

3

"So when did you see him last?" John asked.

The old man had been talking for an hour, but hadn't really told John anything he didn't know already about his grandfather. The men's friendship had been well recorded elsewhere, and although Blacklaw's anecdotes were as funny and witty as John could have hoped for, that wasn't what he'd come all this way to hear.

"Ah," Blacklaw said. "So now we come to it. You want to know about the mysterious end?"

David Blacklaw and Hugh Fraser had broken records together as young men, back in the fifties and sixties, when there were still records to be broken. They had sailed everywhere that could be sailed, climbed most things there were to be climbed, and walked across deserts that had never previously been traversed. They became celebrities in the days before it almost became a dirty word. And they had done it all in style, smoking and drinking—and wenching—their way around the world and into the hearts of the public, which followed their adventures avidly through Fraser's dry yet witty reports, sold to as many papers and magazines as would have them. His eye for a good photograph had also played its part—some of Hugh's black-and-white images had passed into popular culture as iconic depictions of those carefree years. Blacklaw and Fraser were the talk of the town, their fifteen minutes of fame stretching for almost a decade, with not even the whiff of a scandal.

And then suddenly in 1968 it had all stopped—as if switched off like a light bulb. No more reports came from Fraser's pen—indeed, the man was only seen in public once more, in a public bar in Edinburgh. He'd died suddenly in his sleep shortly after that, more than a decade before John was born, and the family never spoke of him. All John knew of the man was what he'd gleaned from the public image—that was all anyone seemed to know.

Now John wanted to know more—needed to know, for if he could ferret out the details of his grandfather's death, his proposed book would go from being just another biography to something that might—just might—have a chance of making his name.

He realized he'd been woolgathering and looked up.

Blacklaw smiled across the fireplace at him.

"I've seen that same look before," the old man said. "In Hugh—ambition, he called it. To me it often looked perilously close to greed. And in the end, it was that which killed him."

John sat forward in his chair. "You're right—I came for that part of the story—my father said heart attack, but I always got the impression he had hid something from me. You'll tell me—you'll tell me how it all ended for the two of you?"

The old man looked suddenly tired, and the color drained from his cheeks.

"It has never really ended," he said, barely more than a whisper. "But I am too tired to tell you—not today. It still touches a raw nerve, even all these years later. Perhaps after dinner, we might share some liquor and I'll pretend it's the old days again. But not now—not so soon after seeing your face."

Blacklaw picked up a bell from the chair-side table and rang twice. The butler was at his shoulder in seconds, helping the old man to his feet. The tartan rugs dropped to the floor. John had been right about Blacklaw's legs—they looked pencil-thin even under his trousers, barely enough to support the man. Blacklaw pushed himself upright with a grimace of pain, and held to the butler's arm as they shuffled across the room.

He turned as they reached the door.

"Dinner at eight," Blacklaw said. "No need to dress up. And I've left you something over on the library table—I think you'll find it interesting, and it will give us something else to talk about over a drink this evening."

John managed to contain himself until the butler and the old man were out of sight, then almost tripped over his feet in his haste to cross the library to the table.

It was a photo album, the cover slightly faded as if overexposed to sunlight at some past date, the leather cracked in several places. There were over a hundred pages at a guess, each with two, sometimes three photographs slipped inside the clear plastic sleeve. His own face looked back at him from many of the images. There was Granddad Hugh on top of a mountain, or sunburned and shirtless in a rowboat, or sitting on a camel with the Sphinx in the background—none of them were images he had ever seen before, although he had seen many similar ones.

One in particular caught his eye—the two young men smiling broadly, arms around each other's shoulders, mugging it up for the camera with the tumbled ruins of a

… lying, fully naked, spread-eagled on a stone floor, atop a painted pentagram.

jungle temple in the background, almost as an afterthought.

He took the album back to the fireside chair and sat with it in his lap, flicking through his granddad's history.

In places it was like a pictorial history of the fifties and sixties. There were plenty of famous people along the way—Monroe, Einstein, Jagger, Gargarin, Twiggy and most of the England World Cup winning team among them. But the only constants, almost always side by side, were Blacklaw and Fraser—"Black and Tan" as the papers of the day had affectionately dubbed them.

John realized as he looked through the pictures that they were in chronological order—the earliest being grainy black and white, the lads barely out of University, bright-eyed and ready for a laugh. The middle section of the album was in full garish sixties color, although the men seemed somewhat soberly dressed by the standards of that decade. After the blocks of color John was surprised when the last few pages of the album contained a collection of more black-and-white prints, some of them almost too murky to make out any detail.

They had all been taken in a dark room—it looked more like a vault—or a dungeon, for there were manacles and chains hanging from rough walls. The photographs showed both Blacklaw and Fraser in varying degrees of undress. They seemed to be dancing, both together and with a series of young—some of them very young—almost naked women. For a few seconds John wondered whether he was looking at an orgy. If so, it was most definitely blackmail material, and he wondered whether he was looking at the thing that had killed both men's careers so quickly and effectively.

The last page of the book showed John's grandfather lying, fully naked, spread-eagled on a stone floor, atop a painted pentagram. There were two photographs—a long shot showing the body lying on the ritual circle and the second a close-up of Hugh Fraser's face.

He was staring, dead-eyed, straight up, but he had a broad smile on his face

4

It was dark when Carole woke, and for the first few seconds she could not remember where she was or how she had gotten there. She lay still for several seconds, letting reality fill in around her sleep-addled mind. It was the sound of the rain on the window that finally allowed her to click back into her proper time and place.

Welcome to Scotland.

There was no sign that John had returned yet. She had the bed to herself, and that was usually a time for her to luxuriate and spread out, but she felt too nauseous. When she laid her head back on the pillow she started to feel dizzy, and as she swung herself out of the soft bed her head spun as if she'd overindulged in too much booze.

What do they put in their cakes up here?

She stumbled her way to the bathroom, barking her shin hard on the bedside cabinet on the way before finally, by fumbling around at the side of the door, managing to switch on a light. She turned on the faucet, and was dismayed to see that the water seemed to be almost orange in color for a while until, with a gurgle and much clanking in the aged plumbing, it ran clearer. She still wouldn't have liked to drink any of it, but it would do for a quick wash and spruce up. She checked her watch and was surprised to find it was only five-thirty; she felt like she'd slept for hours.

She splashed water on her face and stared hard at herself in the mirror above the sink. It wasn't like her to fall asleep in the afternoon. Then again, it wasn't like her to stuff her face with cakes and sweet fancies in the afternoon either.

This place is getting to me.

She heard floorboards creak in the bedroom beyond the door. John had returned, probably creeping in thinking that she might be asleep.

"It's about time," she said and went through. "Where the hell have you been?"

The room was empty—but it felt like someone had just been there. She couldn't put her finger on it. Maybe it was the hint of a smell of heather, or a warmer patch over by the wardrobe mirror as if something had just been standing there, breathing—or even the indentation in the bedclothes that seemed to have been made by a bigger frame than hers.

"Hello?" she said.

There was no answer. She fumbled around the wall until she found a switch and light flooded the room. She was quite alone—but she looked over at the wardrobe just in time to see a patch of condensation at head-height shrink and dissipate, as if retreating from the light.

She threw open the door to the outside landing, ready to scream—only to see John outside, his hand just reaching for the door handle.

"Hi, sweetheart," he said. "I was trying not to wake you."

She pummeled her fists against his chest, but felt too weak to work herself up into a righteous rage.

"Don't do it again. You really scared me," she replied, and fell into his arms.

She felt better after a hot bath, even although the water was still that peculiar orange color, the legacy of getting the supply from a reservoir on a peat bog, John said. He sat on the tub's edge as she soaked, and told her of his conversation with the old man, and of the photo album.

"So you were right?" she said, her interest piqued. "There was some kind of scandal—or threat of one?"

"It certainly looks that way from the photos. I don't know whether Blacklaw will let me use any of them—but he must have shown them to me for a reason. Maybe we'll find out over dinner."

"If the old man turns up—what age is he anyway? He looks pretty frail."

"He was born in the mid-thirties, I think, so he'll be around eighty. He looks even older, I know, but he seems to have been ill for a while. We shouldn't worry about that. I'm sure the staff know how to look after him."

"When they're not looking after themselves, you mean?" Carole replied. "Just get the job done and we can go home—this place reminds me too much what's in store for both of us down the road a way."

John nodded.

"I know what you mean. Let's hope the dinner isn't equally as tired."

Dinner turned out to be a most pleasant surprise. They had a thick soup with fresh bread, followed by salmon, potatoes and greens, all which tasted fresh and vibrant, and a pudding of a sticky treacle sponge that John wolfed down with gusto, but reminded Carole too much of her earlier excesses. She pushed it aside and John finished it off.

Their host had barely picked at his own food and seemed scarcely awake. Conversation had been sparse during the meal itself, and Carole foresaw a long dull evening ahead. But the old man perked up when they rose from the table and went through to sit by the fire in the library.

Like John earlier, Carole was struck dumb by the place as soon as she entered. The swirl of the staircases, the sturdy aged wood of the shelving and the glorious array of books stacked high up into the rafters made the room a thing of beauty she could only stand and gape at in admiration.

Blacklaw raised a laugh at her reaction.

"It gets to most everybody that way on their first visit. If you are not moved by the sheer loveliness of this place, then I am afraid you have no soul—at least none that I care to speak to."

The butler brought a decanter and three glasses and poured a stiff drink for each of them before leaving the tray on a small table between the chairs. He lit a thin cigar for Blacklaw before leaving the three of them alone with only the cracking of the fire and the drumming of rain on the roof high above as company.

"I have sat here alone for many years now," the old man said. "It is nice to have some young company around the house, for McKinnon can be a fusty old stick at times, and his spouse rarely says a word—at least not outside of the kitchen."

He sucked on the cigar, and took in a long drag of smoke that he didn't let out, as if his tissues were swallowing it up in lieu of food.

Carole took a sip of her drink. It was Scotch, something she wasn't really partial to, but this one was smooth, slightly peaty, with a hint of summer flowers—indeed, it tasted like sunshine and warm days, and she took to it with some gusto.

Blacklaw smiled, and took a sip from his own glass.

"Scotch and a cigar—simple pleasures for a simple life. And a far cry from the old days when it would have been all caviar, champagne and dancing girls. But this will do nicely for my dotage. It's our local single malt—made upstream, in the hills. This barrel is forty years old—laid down not long after Hugh himself was. It all seems so long ago now."

Carole was surprised to see tears in the old man's eyes. John leaned forward—she knew what he wanted to get the old man talking about—but she couldn't bring herself to cause such pain to their host. She put a hand on John's arm.

"Let's leave the questions until tomorrow, shall we?"

John looked from her, to Blacklaw, and back again. She thought he might argue the case, but there was no arguing with the fact that Blacklaw was in no fit state to talk for very long.

Instead, and to his credit, John took up the bulk of the conversation.

"I meant to say earlier, I'm very pleased to meet you, Mr. Blacklaw. I've seen photographs, of course, and some of the old documentaries, but it is a pleasure to meet you in person. According to my dad, you were the nearest thing Granddad had to a brother."

"I'm afraid I lost touch with your family many years ago," the old man replied. "Time and distance can do terrible things to any relationships, and ours was already soured by…" He let the sentence drift off. "But tell me of happier times. Were you brought up in the house in Kent?"

John brought the old man up to date on his family history.

"I am so sad that I lost touch. But I remember your father,"

Blacklaw said softly after a while. "He can't have been much more than ten the last time I saw him—a quiet wee boy who wouldn't say boo to a goose."

John nodded. "That was Dad—anything for a quiet life. I think he rebelled against Hugh's extravagant nature."

Blacklaw laughed at that until he started coughing and was forced to stop.

"Extravagant is one way to put it, I suppose. You saw the photographs?"

John nodded.

"I have decided I will indeed tell you the story behind them—but not tonight. Such a tale needs the cold light of day to dispel the darkness. It can wait until morning."

As if in agreement, something fluttered high above in the rafters. Blacklaw saw Carole looking.

"Bats in the belfry, I'm afraid," he said, and cackled. "It comes to us all with age."

For the first time, she wondered whether the old man might not be completely sane.

Blacklaw's stamina did not last long after that. They finished off their drinks while Blacklaw smoked the cigar down to a stub, then he rang for the butler. McKinnon was at the old man's side in seconds, helping him up out of the chair. When John and Carole stood as he rose, he motioned them back to their seats.

"Stay and enjoy the *uisge*," he said. "I get precious little joy out of it myself these days, and someone really should. I'll see you at breakfast around nine, if that's all right by you."

Not waiting for an answer he left, clinging onto the butler like a drowning man clutching a life belt.

John lifted the decanter.

"What do you say—a nightcap?"

Her earlier nausea seemed to have passed, but she still felt a chill when she thought of how she'd allowed herself to get frightened in the bedroom. She held out her glass for him to pour, and motioned for more when John looked like stopping.

"If I'm to get to sleep in this place, I'll need some false courage."

John smiled.

"Don't tell me it's got you spooked already?"

She hadn't gone into detail of what she'd felt earlier—it had sounded silly enough inside her head without having to give voice to it. But she'd already resolved not to leave John's side during this visit—not in the dark at any case.

Whatever was overhead fluttered again, louder than before, and with enough force to disturb some dust and send it showering down toward them. Carole tried to peer into the shadows above, but couldn't see any movement. She downed the liquor fast, enjoying the warm heat of it as it hit her stomach—but it didn't dispel the cold chill in her spine as she followed John back upstairs to the bedroom.

5

John couldn't sleep. Carole had hit the pillow and been gone almost immediately, but John lay on his back, watching the play of shadow in the room, which was considerably darker than he was used to in London. There were no streetlights here, and no passing cars to throw headlights across the walls. Rain continued to rat-a-tat against the windows, and the main source of light was what little came under the door from the hallway outside. And soon even that was gone as someone—probably the butler—switched off the landing lights.

He *needed* this story. He hadn't told anyone—not even Carole—just how much he wanted it. Since he'd decided to be a writer—more than a decade ago now and in what felt like another lifetime—he'd been looking for the big one, the break that would lead to the high life, name in lights, fortune and glory stuff. At an intellectual level he knew that those kinds of deals were all too rare, but emotionally he felt it like a pain in his gut. And when those deals did come along, they mostly went on ghostwritten celebrity exposes—or on celebrity biographies. Hugh Fraser's star might have faded since his heyday in the sixties, but he was still sufficiently known for any new information about his sudden death to be newsworthy. John was banking on it. But first he had to tease out what Blacklaw knew, and the glacial speed at which that was proceeding was enough to have him stifling a scream.

The house fell quiet and the darkness got deeper still, but still sleep evaded him. It was the photographs—that last black-and-white series in the crypt—he could not get the images out of his mind. It was all he could do to stop himself from barging into the old man's bedroom and demanding some answers as to what had been going on.

Instead he tried to distract his racing mind with games and puzzles while lying on his back staring at the dark, working out complex square roots, or trying to come up with cast or crew connections between disparate movies or television shows.

All that served to do was keep him awake longer.

He had no way of measuring the passing of time beyond counting the beats of his heart, and on his first attempt he lost track of the total at somewhere over a thousand when his mind returned again to the photographs.

Finally he realized that he was wide awake. Sleep was even further away than it had been when he'd crawled beneath the covers. Carole moaned and punched her pillow, but didn't wake as he rolled out of bed and went to the bathroom. He closed the door behind him and stood, staring into the mirror for long seconds.

There was a thud from the bedroom, and he expected to go through to see Carole getting up. But she was still asleep, showing no signs of having moved. The thud came again, and this time he identified the source—it came from the window, as if someone was rapping softly on it from the outside.

But we're fifteen feet up at least.

He pulled back the curtains and looked out, but it was too dark to see anything but the rain. There was no recurrence of the sound so he shrugged it off—it might have been only a bird, or a bat, lost in the dark and inclement weather. Blacklaw's words of earlier came back to him.

Bats in the belfry.

He dressed quickly and quietly and slipped out of the door into the hallway. He was making for the library, in the hope that the butler might have left the decanter and glasses there. A stiff drink might be enough to calm his racing thoughts and let him finally get some sleep.

The landing was in complete darkness. Dim, diffuse light came from high above where rain lashed against a domed skylight. Somewhere down on the ground floor yellowish lamplight showed under a door, but the rest was just dark and darker shadows.

He was starting to question his decision to leave the bedroom.

Haven't you seen any movies?

In the end it was the thought of the Scotch more than anything that got him moving. He found his way to the staircase mostly by touch, running his hand along the warm mahogany of the banister. He took the stairs slowly, mindful that they were both steep and uncarpeted. The third from the bottom creaked loudly and echoed around him. He waited to see if anyone would come to investigate, but quiet quickly fell again.

He made his way quickly across the large open hallway. The library door was open, and the embers of the fire showed him his way. It was only once he was in the doorway that he thought of switching on a light. He found two switches by the side of the bookshelves. The first lit up the whole library from top to bottom, but the sudden glare seemed too garish to his dark-acclimatized eyes, so he settled for the second option, which lit three small lamps on the wall over the fireplace and lent the fireside area a cozy, reddish glow.

To his delight, the whisky decanter and glasses were still on the table between the chairs. He went across to the library table, fetched the photograph album, and returned to help himself to a large measure of the fine single-malt.

He sat in Blacklaw's chair at first, but the padding and upholstery had molded itself so well to the old man's body contours that it was a form of torture for anyone else to attempt to relax in it. He went back to the chair he'd sat in earlier, and dragged it back closer to the embers of the fire, a bulwark against the coldness of the night that was winning the battle for the soul of the room.

Any discomfort he might have felt was quickly forgotten as he sipped at the Scotch and lost himself again in the pictorial history of his grandfather's life.

He found one picture that brought back a memory he'd forgotten he had. Hugh and Blacklaw stood posing with a bear—a live, full-sized grizzly, up on its hind legs, standing behind them. Both men—and the bear—seemed to be smiling.

He'd seen the picture before—it was one of the few his dad had a copy of in an album that was rarely opened. John had found it when he was no more than ten years old, and often sneaked a look at it when Dad was out of the house. As a lad he'd often thought of that bear, and how they'd got the picture without being eaten. Seeing it again brought his childhood flooding back, and it was with those memories that he drifted, falling down into sleep.

He woke sometime later with a start, sloshing whisky onto

his lap, and jumping again as the photo album fell to the floor with a loud thud. He sat in almost total darkness, just the dying, barely red of the coals to tell him he was still in the library. He might have slept for ten minutes or three hours—he had no way of knowing. He rescued the whisky glass—thankfully he'd only lost a thimbleful at most—and was trying to feel his way to where he could place it on the table when he heard a fluttering high above.

Bats in the belfry.

But it didn't sound like bats or pigeons—it sounded more like someone scrambling for purchase on the roof, feet sliding on wood, fingers—and fingernails—grasping for a hold.

"Hello?" John said softly, and immediately felt foolish, realizing he had no clue what he might do if anyone actually answered.

The sound got louder—it seemed to be coming from inside the library itself now—and was getting closer.

John stood and tried to get his bearings. Not only was the library light switched off, but the door through to the hallway had been closed. He had a bad moment when he thought he was trapped, then he saw, barely visible, a lighter patch where some light seeped under the door.

He headed in that direction.

The scrambling got louder, almost frantic. There was a thud on the balcony almost directly above him, then another. It took John a second to figure out what it was—books were being dislodged from the shelves, knocked from their position by whatever was up there—and it was very close now. He heard breathing, a thick watery gurgle that sounded like a sick person attempting to laugh.

"Hello?" John said again, and was dismayed to hear the tremor and whine in his voice. He finally reached the door and put his hand on the handle. It felt too cold to the touch, but it turned when he put pressure on it. That small act of normality seemed to lend him some strength.

"This isn't funny. This isn't funny at all."

The scrambling got louder still, mere feet from him now. A book fell from above to thud at John's feet, then another.

"That's quite enough."

John reached out and threw on both light switches.

The library fell quiet and still.

Two books lay at John's feet, but there was no sign of any other disturbance. He looked up, but all he could see were dark shadows high in the rafters. He moved the fallen books with his foot, half expecting some kind of attack, but they were just books.

He slid them aside to leave them at the side of the door, made his way quickly out into the hall and closed the library door quietly behind him.

A minute later he was back in the bedroom, listening to Carole's gentle snoring, and wondering whether he'd imagined the whole thing.

6

John was quiet, almost withdrawn, in the morning and looked like he'd had a bad night. But he waved away Carole's concerns as they shared the cramped bathroom mirror over their morning ablutions.

"I'm fine," he said, and gave her a smile that didn't quite reach his eyes. "You know what I'm like trying to sleep in a new place."

It was more than that—she saw it in his eyes—but she didn't push him. There had been too many rows recently, from both sides, and it wouldn't do to start a new one up in a place where neither of them had a chance to escape.

As for herself, Carole felt much better now that she was rested. She'd slept all through the night, having been only vaguely aware that John had got up—and stayed up for a while—at some point. There was no more recurrence of strange noises and the room, now that she was used to the sounds and feel of the place, actually felt more welcoming and homely than any hotel they might otherwise had stayed in. She was looking forward to breakfast—and maybe coffee afterwards with more of the highland fancies.

The front room felt chilly—the two-bar electric fire was

doing little to heat the high-ceilinged area, and much of the heat it produced seemed to be getting sucked straight up the chimney in the huge fireplace. Carole was glad she'd decided on jeans and thick socks—comfort over style was definitely going to be the order of the day in this place. At least the view out of the window was better than the day before, but not by much. Fog had replaced the rain, and wafted in billowing sheets across the bog, alternately showing and hiding the muddy pools and stunted grasses.

John saw her looking.

"We should get out for a stroll later, if the rain stays off," he said.

She nodded absent-mindedly. A stroll was the last thing on her mind. The room might be cold, but she had a feeling it was positively balmy compared to what it would be like out on the moor.

McKinnon had arrived in the doorway, with that almost magical knack he had been showing of knowing exactly when he was needed.

"Will that be the full Scottish breakfast for two?" he asked.

John looked at Carole and smiled.

"Time to let the belt out a notch, I think—but when in Rome ..."

They ordered the full breakfasts and sat down. There were only the two of them at the table for almost half an hour, in which time they ate a small mountain of food between them—porridge first, then bacon, eggs, black pudding and sausages with a heap of toast and as much coffee as they wanted. By the time the butler showed Blacklaw to the top seat, Carole was quite full.

"Apologies," the old man said. "It takes me a while to get going some mornings, especially when it's a tad damp. I hope

McKinnon has been looking after you?"

Carole smiled through the last mouthful of toast she was going to be able to manage.

Blacklaw once again barely touched the small helping of breakfast that was brought for him, although he did take two cups of black coffee, after which he was distinctly more animated. He perked up even more when the butler brought him a tray containing a lighter and a single cigarette.

He looked at Carole and smiled. For the first time she saw the younger man he had been, and could well imagine that he had indeed melted many hearts. "Capable of dropping knickers at two hundred yards" was the phrase John had quoted from an old newspaper clipping, and seeing him smile now, she could well believe it.

"Forgive an old man's indulgence," Blacklaw said as he lit the cigarette. "I'm only allowed one of these and one cigar a day, so I must make the most of them."

He sucked in a lungful of smoke, and as before, almost none came back out. Then he let out a satisfied sigh.

"I do miss smoking. I know I'd be looked on as a pariah these days, but when I was young it was almost compulsory, and it's a pleasure I am loath to deny myself in these last months."

"Nonsense," Carole said. "You've got years in you yet, surely?"

That got her another smile, one filled with sadness.

"I wish it were true," he replied. "Although my doctor seems to think otherwise. But come, let us not ruin the morning talking about me." He turned to speak to John. "Now, young Fraser, I suppose you expect a story?"

"As long as you feel up to it…" John said, and Blacklaw smiled again.

"It's now or never," he replied. "I might not get too many more mornings in which to tell it. And if anyone deserves to hear it, it is you, my boy. But it will take some time—and you really should take notes, for there is a lot of detail you might want to check on later."

John nodded.

"I came prepared," he said, and took out his pocket recorder. "Do you mind?"

Blacklaw did not seem to understand what was being asked, until John showed him the purpose of the recorder, which was no bigger than a cigarette packet. Once he knew what it was, Blacklaw laughed.

"Your granddad would have loved it—he loved gadgets—although in our day the high point of technology was his portable reel-to-reel player. Remind me to tell old McKinnon later—there's a box of tapes somewhere that you should have. But we are digressing already, and I haven't even started. Let me take you back, to nineteen sixty-eight, and a night in a bar in Edinburgh."

There was a click as John started recording; then the only sound was the whisper of the old man's voice.

7

"We were rather famous at one time, you know?

"It wasn't something we sought out—at least not at first. As you know, your Granddad and I met at Edinburgh University in the early fifties, and we hit it off straight away. Soon we were spending our weekends in the hills climbing, and our weekdays working our way through the female student population. Oh, don't look so shocked—sex wasn't invented in the sixties.

"After graduation we put off gainful employment by taking ourselves off to the Alps in search of higher climbs and more exotic women. And it was there that fame fell into our laps—we rescued, then bedded, three girls on the Matterhorn, our pictures made the French and Italian papers. We soon realized we rather liked the attention, and away we went, on fifteen years of adventure and debauchery.

"And although that all brought rewards and riches beyond our dreams, it was never really enough for Hugh. There was always going to be another mountain to climb, another desert to cross, another woman to conquer.

"But by the late sixties, our star was on the wane. We were well into our thirties by then. Older chaps like us had to make way for younger men with long hair and loud music, drugs and outlandish clothes. The world turned, and we were too slow in turning with it. You have to understand that Hugh and I—myself in particular—were very much the products of a war and immediate post-war upbringing. We were stiff-upper-lip types in a world that was quickly passing us by. Our accents were suddenly too "posh," our activities, while risqué, were not sufficiently salacious, but mostly we were just getting too long in the tooth, in London particularly, for a culture that was now worshipping at the altar of youth.

"For my part, I would have been happy by '68 to let it all go. The constant traveling was wearing away at me, and I yearned for hearth and home in the Highlands. We were set up for life, I had already bought this place for a song when the previous laird died, and I was looking forward to a long, quiet retirement. Hugh, of course, had other ideas, and that weekend in Edinburgh was meant to persuade me that there was still life in the old dogs, even after all our previous adventures.

"When I met him in the Café Royal, he was as excited as I'd seen him in years. I expected him to have plans in place for some new adventure in a far-flung locale, but as it turned out, his plans were for something much closer to home.

"We hadn't been in the Royal since our student days, and it was something of a homecoming for us. We drank beer and reminisced about the old days for a while before Hugh got to the point. It being a weekday afternoon, and not in the middle of tourist season, the place was almost empty, and the sound Hugh made as he dropped a book on the table echoed in the high-ceilinged bar like a gunshot.

"'I've got it, Blackie,' he said.

"As I said, it was a book—and it looked old. Beyond that I couldn't tell, as he refused to let me look closer when I leaned to drag it across the table toward me.

"'Not yet,' he said. 'Not until I've told you. I think I've

found a way to keep us relevant.'

"Now, I had never stopped feeling relevant—in fact, I had never started—but Hugh was in one of his excited-puppy moods and my only options were to leave him alone in the bar or to listen.

"My curiosity got the better of me. I stayed, and I listened.

"'I got the idea from a blasted television program, of all things,' Hugh started. 'You know how the youth are now involved in strange music, magic and all that nonsense? Well, why don't we give them some—why don't we give them a great big dose of it?'

"It was only then that he pushed the book over the table to me. I could see immediately that it was rather old, leather-bound, and in a fragile condition, to say the least. The top right quadrant had suffered severe water damage at some time in its life, and the lower portion of the spine was starting to fray and separate from the main book. Any writing that might once have been on the cover itself was long since worn and faded away, and I feared it might fall apart in my hands should I grip it too tightly.

"I opened it gingerly and read an inscription inside the jacket.

"*Ye Twelve Concordances of ye Redde Serpent. In wych is succinctly and methodically handled the stone of ye philosophers, his excellent effectes and admirable vertues; and, the better to attaine to the originall and true meanes of perfection, inriched with Figures representing the proper colors to lyfe as they successively appere in the practice of this blessed worke.*

"'What in blazes is this nonsense?' I asked.

"'Nonsense indeed,' Hugh said, smiling. 'Some kind of medieval Scottish alchemy text, I believe. I found it in a shop in the Cattlemarket. But it scarcely matters—it is no more than our McGuffin, our plot device to get things going, a purpose for which it should do nicely.'

"'Do for what?' I asked, fearing the answer.

"'For our comeback show, of course,' Hugh said, and laughed. 'We are going to raise some hell for the kids.'

"Over the course of a few more beers Hugh laid out his plan. As was often the case with his more outlandish suggestions, he steamrollered my initial skepticism with his force of will and sheer enthusiasm, such that by the end of the afternoon I was quite sold on the idea that he might be onto something big this time.

"His scheme, on the face of it, was a remarkably simple one—we would make a documentary—and, we hoped, a full series of them—investigating the supernatural from our unique viewpoint as travelers and adventurers.

"'Who better than us?' he said. 'We have trodden where angels fear to tread, we have conquered things that were said to be unconquerable—let us tilt at some new windmills. If we are to go down into oblivion, let us at least go down fighting.'

"As I said, he had me most of the way convinced. I agreed that we should take the matter forward with our contacts in the BBC, and told Hugh he could get the ball rolling—I was on board.

"That was when he told me that he wanted to use my house—this house, for our first investigation.

"'It's perfect, Blackie,' he said, in that way he had that brooked no argument. 'It's spooky and old and full of atmosphere—and we don't have to get a camera crew and cast to travel abroad. I can see it all in my head already.

And I've found just the right spell to put the wind up the unwashed masses on the television.'

"'What do you mean, spell? Like black magic—hocus-pocus?'

"'Precisely,' he replied. 'We use the ritual as set out in the book, add in some theatricality and dramatic music and such, and build up the tension to breaking point. Then, of course, nothing at all will happen. We'll all have a jolly good laugh, and spend the rest of the program explaining why it failed. Science and rationality wins, superstition is dispelled and we all—especially the two of us—get our profiles raised back to where we should be.'

"As I say, he had me convinced, and I could foresee no risks in what he meant to attempt. In all our travels and high adventures we had never once come across anything that could not be explained by science and common sense. Neither of us believed that this time would be any different.

"Both of us were very wrong."

Blacklaw stopped as he was hit by a sudden coughing fit that brought flecks of blood to his lips, but he waved Carole away when she started to get out of her chair to go to his aid.

"I'm busted up inside, my dear," he said once he had calmed. "The lungs are shot, my guts can only hold enough food to feed a mouse, and I've got about as much muscle as a newborn chick. But I'm good for a wee bit longer yet. Let me tell my tale—it feels good to get it out, after all these years, and we need to get to the nub of the matter before I get too tired to continue.

"I left Hugh outside the Café Royal late that afternoon

and did not see him for another two weeks, but in that time he managed to persuade the BBC to give us a chance. He sent handwritten letters relating our progress, which all went remarkably smoothly, and around a month later, we were ready to go.

"We set up in the cellar downstairs—right beneath where we are sitting here. I had some extra chains and manacles added for effect, and McKinnon—who was also a sprightly young thing back then—had to cart several truck loads of accumulated junk up and out onto the drive before we had room for filming.

"I remember most clearly that the girls Hugh had brought up from London whined the whole time during rehearsals about the cold and the damp, and the wine cellar's contents took a pounding that cost me a pretty penny to replenish. But Hugh was happy—more than that, he was energized in a way I had not seen him for several years.

"The night before filming we were sitting in these very same chairs having a drink and a smoke when he showed me the passage in the book—the ritual he intended to perform. There was an illuminated drawing there that drew my gaze.

"*CALX* was the heading. The drawing showed a naked young man, bound to a burning wheel by hands and feet in a figure X. The wheel was set on a remote patch of land. It looked to be a barren heath on a high plateau that would have borne a striking resemblance to the view out of my front window if the mountains had been a tad higher in these parts. The fire from the wheel was starting to consume the man's arms and legs, and flames were taking hold in his hair. But despite the torment, the bound figure was smiling broadly.

"Hugh tapped at the picture.

"'This is the lasting image I want the viewers to remember.

It is from Greek mythology. Zeus punished Ixion, a poet, for trying to seduce the goddess Hera. For his presumption Ixion was bound to a perpetual wheel of fire. But the poet had seen the face of the goddess, and although he was bound in eternal pain, he was also eternally happy. That is something there's a lot of in the Concordances—duality. Everything can be seen from two angles. Everything has at least two meanings. But for our purposes it is simple. We won't be mentioning the Greek stuff at all. We'll have the wheel, some chanting, some drums and some girls in their underwear—that'll get the viewing figures rocketing if nothing else.'

"'So it's really all going to be a sham?' I asked.

"Hugh smiled.

"'Not all of it—as I told you back in the Royal, I intend to use the chant as detailed in the book—but we'll both know that's just for verisimilitude. Don't worry, old boy. A couple of hours of filming; then the lads will get it off to London and we'll be back on top before the summer's out.'

"We went down into the cellar the next night."

"It all started smoothly enough.

"The cellar was dashed cold, and the girls suddenly shy about shedding their clothes, but Hugh was not to be argued with. He took control of the whole shoot and orchestrated it with the bravado of a top conductor. As I said before—he seemed energized by the whole affair. We soon had a chant ringing and echoing around us—the acoustics of the cellar being such that it often sounded like there were many more voices than our own raised in the chorus. You have seen the photographs, so you have some idea as to what went on, but what the photos can't describe is the tension—the electricity—in the air. Drums beat loudly, the girls danced, and the chanting rose to frenzied heights. Hugh laid himself down, naked on the circles we had painted on the floor and shouted out the final line of the ritual.

"'*Dhumna Ort!*'

"There was a crack, and a flash, and all the electrics in the house shorted out at once, leaving us in total blackness.

"As you can imagine there was a certain degree of panic, but between McKinnon and myself we managed to get the crew and the girls back up into the light—it was only then I noticed that Hugh wasn't with us.

"I took a lantern back down into the cellar and called his name—but Hugh would never answer me again.

"He lay in the center of the circle where I had last seen him—eyes staring sightlessly upward, a broad smile on his face."

8

"He died here? In the cellar?" John said. "Why wasn't I ever told?"

"You'll have to ask your father that," Blacklaw said. "Your grandmother knew the story well enough, although she never spoke to me again after the funeral. She was a close-mouthed woman, though, and it may be that she took the story with her to her grave—your own father might never have been told."

"Okay—I understand that the family might want to bury such a story—but what about the media? And what about your legacy?"

Blacklaw laughed, then had to stop again when a cough brought blood to his lips.

"The media didn't want any trouble," he said. "'*BBC crew in black magic orgy death*' was not the kind of headline they were thinking of when they sent their people up here. As for legacy—all I wanted after Hugh passed was to be left alone to mourn."

"So it was covered up?" John asked.

Blacklaw seemed almost too tired to reply.

"Of course it was," he said. His voice was throaty and little more than a croak. "It wasn't just the BBC who had a stake in us. We had publishers, agents and newspapers all earning from our exploits. A scandal could not—would not—be tolerated. But it wasn't really a cover-up—after a while people just stopped talking about us. How do you say it these days? We fell off the radar."

"Quite a fall," John said.

"Well, I may have helped by jumping," Blacklaw replied, and smiled. "I got my wish of retirement and moved permanently to this house. We gave Hugh a quiet funeral, and I settled down to a much simpler life while the world turned."

He picked up a small bell from the table and rang.

The butler, McKinnon, appeared at Blacklaw's side to help him rise from the table, as if he'd been standing just outside the door waiting for the call.

"Now, if you will excuse me," Blacklaw said, clearly struggling to get the words out. "I have talked more this morning than I have all year. I need to lie down. But I think I have left you more than enough to mull over. If I am well enough to get downstairs, we shall speak again this evening."

Once again the old man and the butler shuffled out of the room, leaving John and Carole in a dumfounded silence.

"Do you think he's telling the truth?" Carole asked.

John leaned over and switched off the recorder before answering.

"He's got no reason to lie to us—at least none that I can see. It's a hell of a story though—and just the sort of thing I need. If he'll let me use the photos, we could be looking at a big seller here. There could even be a bidding war for the rights if we play our cards right. Imagine the stir—a naked photo of Hugh Fraser during a Satanic ritual—the Sundays will eat it up and shout for more."

He noticed, too late, that Carole was none too happy with him.

"You'd use your own family that way?"

John nodded.

"Why not? All's fair in this game."

"And what would your parents have thought—would your dad like to have his own father's name dragged through the mud backwards?"

"I hadn't thought of it like that..." John started, but wasn't given time to finish.

"Of course you hadn't. You never do. I'll be upstairs. Leave me alone for a while if you know what's good for you."

She stood, too fast, knocking her chair over with a loud crash, but didn't stop to right it and didn't look back as she left. Any thought of following her was swiftly dispelled by memories of previous arguments—none of which he had come close to winning.

He poured himself some coffee—it was still warm enough to drink, although not piping hot—and took it through to the library.

He'd intended to have another look at the photo album. He'd left it on the floor the night before, but as he entered the room he saw the album was no longer there. Suddenly reminded of his nighttime experience, he looked up to the rafters. Thin sunlight leaked in from a skylight at the highest point. There was no sign of any movement. If there had been even the slightest hint of rustling, John was ready to flee, but the house had fallen quiet again now that breakfast was over, and the thick fog soundproofed it against any external noises. The library was silent and still.

John made his way over to the library table. Someone—McKinnon again, probably—had replaced the photo album in its previous position. It sat on top of two other books—John wondered if they were the same two that had fallen at his feet during the night, then pushed that thought away—he did not need any more reminders of how close he'd come to a screaming funk.

He took the photograph album back to the chair by the fire and sat, lost in thought, going over and over again in his mind what Blacklaw had revealed to him of his grandfather's death.

The photographs at the end of the book fitted Blacklaw's story, but the tale felt unfinished somehow, as if an important piece had been left off the board. John looked closer at the photographs, studying not just the foreground figures, but any detail that could be made out in the background, hoping that something vital might jump out at him and bring the story into focus. Now that he knew they were mere props, the chains and manacles looked slightly cheesy and out of place, and the dancers seemed posed for effect, caught like groups of sculptures in half-embarrassed poses. Even Hugh's naked body on the ritual circle looked too pale—too clean.

He kept staring at the pictures for a good twenty minutes, but it was no use. The flat black-and-whites from more than forty years ago had no more secrets to give up.

I'll need to talk to the old man again.

Given Blacklaw's state of health, he didn't know how much more time he would be allowed. He'd come here hoping for a story that would form the backbone of his biography. What he'd got was stunning, yes, but still not enough to satisfy the current excesses of the media—the photographs only served to emphasize the fact that the story was old—and getting older by the day. He needed more.

After studying the images, he switched on his recorder and played back the interview—or monologue, as it had turned out. Blacklaw's voice sounded even weaker on replay—the whispers of an obviously dying man. Like the photographs, the playback didn't reveal any new secrets—not until it got near the end.

"You have seen the photographs, so you have some idea as to what went on, but what the photos can't describe is the tension—the electricity—in the air. Drums beat louder, the girls danced, and the chanting rose to frenzied heights," Blacklaw said.

And at that, the playback became distorted with banging and hissing sounds, a cacophony of white noise much louder than Blacklaw's voice. It grated on the ears and sent spikes of lancing light dancing in John's eyes, a ten-second assault like standing too close to the stage at a rock concert that rose to a blasting crescendo before cutting off as quickly as it had come. The old man's voice took over again.

"'*Dhumna Ort!*'

The rest of the playback continued normally. John let it play through, then went back to where the white noise had kicked in. He turned the volume of his recorder down to a level where he could stand listening to the cacophony and played back the section, over and over again, listening for anything that might give him a clue as to what he had picked up.

At first he thought it might be no more than a glitch in the recording, a bad section on the solid-state drive that held the

Then he started to hear voices in the sound, a rhythmic chanting …

box's recordings. Then he started to hear voices in the sound, a rhythmic chanting that underpinned the white noise. He tried to use the controls on the side of the box as filters, and found that by turning the treble right down and the bass up to maximum, he could almost discern words.

It sounded like Latin, a deep chanting, like monks at prayer. He played it over and over, trying to discern meaning.

And in answer, something rustled, high in the rafters above.

"You need to hear this," John said two minutes later as he pushed open the bedroom door.

Carole looked him up and down. "I really don't, you know," she said.

It seemed she was still angry with him, but John ploughed on regardless. "Okay—I get it, I'm an insensitive wanker—I agree with you. Now will you listen to this? It's important."

"Important how?"

"I don't rightly know as yet—but just listen, will you?"

He took the recording back to the section where the noise started. Blacklaw's voice whispered back at him again.

"*Drums beat louder, the girls danced and the chanting rose to frenzied heights. Hugh laid himself down, naked on the circles we had painted on the floor and shouted out the final line of the ritual.*

"'*Dhumna Ort!*'

"*There was a crack, and a flash, and all the electrics in the house shorted out at once, leaving us in total blackness.*"

There was no sign of any white noise, no break at all in the flow of Blacklaw's words. He fiddled with the bass and treble controls and played it again, and again but each time there was only the old man's voice on the playback.

9

Carole saw that John was confused—more than that, he looked almost scared.

"What is it?" she said. "What did you want me to hear?"

John sat down hard on the edge of the bed. He shook the recorder, tapping it hard with his hand, then played back the same section again, three times before she asked him to stop.

"You're starting to scare me here. Talk to me, John. Tell me what happened."

He couldn't take his eyes off the recorder.

"I'm starting to scare myself. But it was there. I heard it."

"What was?"

He finally started to talk, telling her about an area of white noise on the recording that might—or might not—have contained some ritual chanting in Latin. He mentioned hearing a rustling in the rafters—then went on to tell her about his experience the night before.

"There's something in that library," he said softly. "I'm sure of it. Something that's not meant to be there."

She wasn't quite sure whether he was being serious. John wasn't a man prone to flights of fancy and had always been dismissive of anything even remotely claiming to be supernatural.

"*Something?* What do you mean by that?"

He was quiet for several seconds before continuing.

"The old man isn't telling us everything he knows. And I mean to get to the bottom of it."

He started to rise but she pulled him back down beside her on the edge of the bed.

"Slow down," Carole replied. "The old man's sick—and probably asleep. What are you going to do—slap him awake and torture him into a confession?"

John slumped against her. She stroked his hair.

"We need to take our time," she said, softly. "You've had a shock—you've just learned how your grandfather died. It's no surprise that you're a bit on edge." She felt him relax at her side—not much, but it was a start. "Let's get outside for a bit—some fresh air might do us both good—and we need to walk off some of that breakfast if we don't want to leave here several pounds heavier than we came."

John had another look at the recorder, than put it down on the bedside table before joining her in dressing for a walk on the moor.

It was getting on for noon as they went out the main door. As soon as they stepped out onto the gravel drive it was immediately obvious that they weren't going to see much in the way of views. The fog clung to the moor like a thick blanket, shifting only slowly, almost languidly, in what little breeze existed and limiting their view to a hundred yards at most. Everything looked washed-out and gray, and John was all for turning straight back inside.

"No, you don't," Carole said, and took John by the arm. "We'll head up the driveway for a bit—it might clear up further along."

She didn't believe it herself—the weather looked to be settled in for a long stay—but she'd been right earlier—they needed some clear air and a fresh perspective, if only to keep them away from each other's throat for a while longer. Besides, it would also keep John from obsessing about what might—or might not—inhabit the high spaces in the library.

They walked arm in arm in silence for several minutes, until John turned for a look back at the house.

It was already mostly obscured by fog, showing only as a darker patch against the gray, a yellow light in one of the windows like a single unblinking eye looking back at them, the opposite window closed, as if winking. Suddenly Carole had an image of the house as the head of some malevolent giant, buried to his neck in the bog, but perfectly happy to be standing there, drinking fog and leering at passing travelers. She wasn't normally prone to morbid thoughts, but it wasn't only John who had gotten more than slightly spooked. She shivered, and gripped John's arm tighter.

"I've been thinking," John said.

"Don't strain yourself, dear," Carole replied, and was glad to get a laugh rather than a grunt in reply.

"No, really," he said. "You're right. It would be too tacky to use old Hugh's death just to sell books. I see that. I just got carried away with the thought of fortune and glory—you know what we writers are like?"

Carole nodded, but didn't speak, as she could see he wanted to continue.

"But I'm right about there being something else going on in that house," he said. "I can feel it in my bones. And whether it's tied to Granddad or not, there's a story in it. You know me well enough to know that I've got a good nose for these things."

She nodded again, remembering celebrations of previous scoops, front-page stories with John's byline, days when he'd been the golden boy of Fleet Street—days that had become few and far between in recent times. The arguments had become more frequent around the time that the stories started drying up. If John had got his teeth into something here in this godforsaken wasteland, then she fully intended to let him have his head—for the benefit of both his sanity and her own.

She gave him a peck on the cheek.

"Go get them, tiger. I've got your back."

That got her another smile, and suddenly this trip didn't seem so bad after all.

They walked along the driveway for another ten minutes, picking their way around the larger puddles and once having to skirt around the edge of the bog itself to get past a dip in the road that had filled with mucky, almost black water. There was no sign of the fog thinning—in fact it got thicker, if anything, and colder against her hands and cheeks. She chose not to complain—John's mood had improved considerably since breakfast, and despite the fog it felt good to be out walking in open ground and away from the house, if only for a short while.

They had been walking in deep silence, like being enveloped in damp candy floss, so they both got a surprise when a loud splash came from their left, from deeper in the bog beyond the bounds of the driveway.

"What the hell was that?" Carole said. She immediately thought of the buried giant again, waggling a buried finger and causing a commotion in the boggy pools. She berated herself for an overactive imagination, and once again gripped John's arm tighter as they stopped and looked towards where they thought the noise had originated.

There was another splash—on the right side of the path this time, and nearer than the last.

"If anything starts howling, leg it," John said, but his attempt at humor fell flat when there was yet another splash. It sounded like it was just at the edge of the fog, barely out of sight.

"There's something out there," Carole said, whispering, in case she gave away their position.

"I'm pretty sure it's nothing that can harm us," John said, but there was a tremor in his voice that belied his bravado. "There are no big predators around here. Just foxes and stoats—stuff like that."

Another loud splash came as he stopped talking, like an exclamation point punctuating his words.

"That's a bloody big fox," Carole said.

They were still trying to peer into the fog when they heard a moan, like the wailing of wind through a drafty window.

"Let's head back," John said, and started to pull her away.

They retreated at speed down the drive. Carole looked back, but saw only shifting fog. John was almost dragging her now, their walk having turned into a jog. They didn't bother avoiding the puddles, splashing their way through even the deeper ones. Carole felt chill water soak around her ankles and seep into her shoes, making each step squelch wetly. It didn't slow her.

She only looked back once more, as the house loomed into view ahead of them.

Later, as they reached the front door of the house and

castigated themselves for getting spooked, she couldn't be sure what she'd seen. It had been little more than a darker smudge in the gray, but it reminded her once again of the hunched figure she'd watched from the window the day before as it trudged disconsolately through the bog.

10

McKinnon, the butler, was already at the door, waiting to take their coats as they squelched in off the moor. They immediately kicked off their shoes and tugged off the heavy socks that were completely saturated with water. The butler took the socks and deposited them in a bucket beside the door.

"I'll have them back to you within the hour," he said. "If you need any dry pairs, just ask. We keep spares for just this eventuality."

The old man looked ready to deal with any eventuality whatsoever, and was calm and unflustered as ever.

"Does anyone else live around here?" John asked as he handed over his jacket.

"No, sir," the butler replied. "Not for almost fifteen miles."

"We heard someone, out on the moor," John said. "Could it have been one of the staff?"

"No, sir," the man said again. "Everybody is accounted for. Perhaps it was a hunter—they sometimes cross the grounds going after a stag."

John saw signs of evasion in the man now, but didn't press it.

Not yet. I still need more background, and it has to come from Blacklaw.

The butler turned away to hang up the coats.

"The Maister asked me to leave some tapes in the library for you, sir," he said. "I believe he informed you of this?"

John nodded, the strange splashing on the moor immediately forgotten at the prospect of exactly the kind of background he'd just been considering.

"I'm going to take a bath and try to get my feet warm," Carole said. "You go and have a rummage through the tapes—they might be just what you are looking for. You can tell me all about it later."

John stopped the butler just as he was walking away.

"Will Mr. Blacklaw be joining us for lunch?"

"I'm afraid not, sir. He was rather tired after breakfast and will not be down until this evening. I will bring a plate of bread, cheese and cold meats to the front room if you wish something?"

John looked at Carole and she nodded.

"I'll be back down in half an hour," she said. "Try to leave some for me."

She gave him a smile that reminded him that the day had been getting better by the moment before their walk, and went upstairs.

John ignored the prospect of food and headed straight for the library.

The box on the library floor looked as though the butler would have needed help to carry it. It was a two-foot cube, and it was filled with tapes for the small reel to reel player that sat nearby on the small coffee table beside the fireside chair.

John sat down and studied the portable player for several

minutes. It had belonged to old Hugh, and was the first thing of his grandfather's that John had knowingly touched. It was also strangely beautiful, in a retro kind of way, in a lurid red '60s plastic with chrome fittings. He ran his hands over the case, studied the microphone—it was polished and worn by use—and made sure that the mechanism was in working order. It ran on 12-volt batteries, and someone—again, McKinnon at a guess—had been thoughtful enough to have them fitted and ready for use.

A quick look at the tapes showed them to be filed in chronological order, with the more recent on top of the box. John ignored the very last one—he'd get to that in his own good time—and chose one that was dated January, 1968. It took some fiddling and cursing to get the tape leaders in place on the tiny player, but once he got the hang of it, John was able to wind the tape onto the spools, and eventually mastered the technique of getting the player functioning.

Seconds later, Hugh Fraser spoke to him from the great beyond.

"I believe I have found a book that will suit my purposes nicely."

John was almost surprised to find that his granddad had a soft but definite Scottish accent. John, and his own parents before him, had grown up in the south of England, but it seemed that Hugh had not strayed too far from his own Scottish roots, despite having left his homeland for "fortune and glory" straight after university.

"When I went in I was still not sure exactly what I was

looking for. I had a giggle when I misread 'Esoterica' as 'Erotica' and nearly walked past the section, but the book caught my eye immediately despite being in rather poor condition compared to its brothers and sisters on the shelves.

"The chap in the shop tried to tell me it was worth two pounds but I haggled him down to nineteen shillings and sixpence, and will consider it well worth the price should it help me in my goal.

"I had a quick flick through it in the shop, and a closer look just before making this recording. It contains several splendid possible visuals, any one of which will look simply stunning on television sets and should provide the appropriate thrills for our intended audience. The book is also filled with the most impenetrable nonsense about antimony, pelicans, red serpents and 'quintessential mercury'—whatever that might be. It purports to be some kind of step-by-step guide for achieving immortality—but I believe I know a more reliable method. Television appearances on the BBC at peak times might not guarantee the survival of the body, but will at least give me peace in the knowledge that our names will live on in the public's memories long after we have passed.

"But the immortality guff is all of little to no import and can be safely ignored. What may prove useful, though, are certain rituals and incantations in the book that I feel could be readily employed to lend verisimilitude to our little charade, especially if we get the setting and tone just right. The people of Britain could do with a good fright on a Saturday after their supper.

"I cannot wait to tell Blackie of my plan—I really do believe this will be the thing to get us back up to where we belong."

At this point the tape hissed, and John thought he might have chosen one that contained merely a fragment, but after ten seconds or so Hugh's voice continued—although this time he sounded distinctly less happy.

"This blasted book has got under my skin. It's damned confounding, full of riddles and double meanings, but I also get the sense that there's something deeper going on here, some meaning that I might fathom if I could only delve deeply enough. I have talked to the producers in the BBC and while they are not completely sold on the idea of my documentary series, they have expressed an interest in a one-off, and are willing to provide a small crew should I find an appropriate location. That should not be a problem—when Blackie showed me round his new place in Scotland, there was a huge, dark cellar—just the place for spooky goings-on. I can see it all in my mind's eye already—the chanting, the dancing, and the chalked magic circles on the floor—all those fans of old Wheatley will lap it up. All I have to do is persuade Blackie—I'm sure he will see that this is the only way forward for us."

The tape hissed—and kept on hissing this time.

John was about to fast-forward to check for more when Carole arrived and demanded that they eat something. He left the tapes in the library and joined her in the dining room for lunch.

11

McKinnon had laid out enough food to feed a small army. There was cold pressed ham, pork pies, handmade sausage rolls, and bread and cheese aplenty.

Carole was soon feeling pleasantly full and relaxed, especially as he'd provided some strong local ale to accompany the buffet. Over John's shoulder she had a clear view of the bay window and the fog-bound moor beyond, but her long, luxurious soak in the bath upstairs had also washed away her foreboding about the splashing sounds on the moor. She felt slightly embarrassed now to think of their rushed flight along the gravel drive. John hadn't brought it up again, so she put it to the back of her mind and concentrated on what he was telling her.

John had kept up a constant chat about his granddad—the story now had complete hold of him. "Black magic, ancient books, rituals, and Black and Tan at the center of it all—he was right. It would have made a great bit of television back in the day—never mind back in the day, it would make a great bit of television now. I wonder if the old man knows what happened to the film. Imagine if it could be found. That wouldn't just be a big story—it would be bloody huge."

She'd seen him like this before on other stories, but he'd never seemed so energized—she presumed it must be the family connection.

"So ask him," Carole replied.

"I intend to. And we need to have a look down that cellar," he said.

"Why? You've seen the photos. And I doubt there's much to see now, all these years later. You heard Blacklaw—he keeps junk down there."

"Kept," John said. "He kept junk down there, before old Hugh died. Who knows what's down there now? If there's a chance that there's anything left from the night it all happened, I have to see it."

"Well then, let's do it now. Old McKinnon should be able to point the way. And he's bound to have a key if the door is locked."

As if by magic, the butler appeared in the doorway.

"I could not help but overhear," he said. "The cellar has indeed not been used since the night in question—it did not seem quite proper. The Maister told me to expect that you would ask about it. Anytime you would like to go down below, the door is the heavy wooden one. It's second on the right at the end of the hall, and I have left it unlocked."

With that, he cleared up the remains of their lunch and left, showing no sign of wanting to accompany them—in fact, he seemed to be in rather a hurry to be gone. Carole felt the first shiver of apprehension.

Maybe this isn't such a good idea after all.

John seemed to have no such qualms.

"So what's it to be," he said, smiling. "Shall we investigate the splashing thing out on the moor again? Or shall we go down into a dank old cellar that hasn't been used since someone died down there? Don't say I never show you a good time."

It was colder out in the hallway, and Carole fetched her outdoor jacket from the rack. It was slightly damp, but kept the worst of the chill breeze out as they headed for the cellar door. It opened after John put his weight into pulling on it, creaking loudly and rasping, wood against stone floor to show a steep set of stone stairs heading down into blackness.

John found a light switch on the wall just inside the doorway and clicked it on. A single bulb gave out barely enough illumination to show them that the steps went down for some distance. The air smelled damp and musty, and a new breeze came up from the darkness and sent a cold whisper past them into the hall at their backs.

"It must be filthy down there. I just had a bath," Carole said. "And this skirt isn't really meant for exploring dank cellars."

John took her hand.

"It can't be far down," he said. "Just try not to touch the walls. We'll be fine. I just want a quick look."

They went down, gingerly at first, then more confidently as it was obvious there was light coming up from below. After twenty steps they reached bottom and looked out over a long vaulted cellar.

If Blacklaw ever had junk stored in the place, it hadn't been for a long time. The room was empty and quiet. Manacles and chains hung from the walls and, directly beneath a fluorescent light strip, the floor was painted. The fading remains of concentric circles ran around a five-pointed star that was itself inlaid with strange squiggles and symbols that Carole did not recognize and had no desire to see any closer.

John seemed to sense her reluctance. He gripped her hand

tighter and stepped forward into the room. It was even colder down here, a damp chill that threatened to seep into Carole's bones and stay for a while. Water dripped somewhere in the shadows and a smell of mold and decay hung heavy in the air.

"There's nothing to see here," she whispered, and was dismayed as the vault took up her voice and sent it back to her as a fading echo.

"I just want a quick look around," John said again, and led her over to the painted circles on the floor. Carole tried not to think about John's granddad, lying there dead and smiling. She still hadn't seen the photographs—but that did not mean she could not imagine the scene. In fact, she could imagine it all too well.

The ritualized markings might have been white at one time, but they were now faded and gray, although they had not been scuffed or defaced in any way. As they got closer to them, Carole felt the chill bite deeper at her ankles, as if she'd just stepped into another puddle, although the floor was dry and dusty when she looked down.

"I don't like this," she said, and once more the echo took her voice and carried it around the vault. And this time it got a reply, a skittering in a dark corner, as if something had taken fright at the sound and was scurrying for cover.

"Come on, John. They've got rats. You know how I feel about rodents."

John looked like he might argue, but the skittering came again, louder this time, and Carole was in no mood to wait for it to come closer. She let go of John's hand and headed for the stairs.

Before she was halfway across the cellar floor, a moan—high and whining and eerily reminiscent of the one they'd heard on the moor—filled the room, echoing and ringing until it seemed that a chorus of voices was raised in unison. The neon light flickered and threatened to go out completely. It got colder fast, Carole's breath condensing in the air.

The shadows shifted in the far corner, the source of the rustling noises. John looked in that direction, then back at Carole. The moaning became a pounding, like a soft drumbeat. The neon light pulsed in time, and as the moaning finally faded, the skittering in the corner once again could be heard, even louder now, much closer.

Finally John had had enough too. He joined Carole in making for the exit. She only just beat him to the stairs, and a minute later they were back up in the hallway, firmly closing the cellar door behind them.

"It's just the wind," McKinnon said several minutes later as he fetched them a pot of strong coffee. "Whatever else could it be?"

"Whatever else indeed?" Carole whispered. She knew one thing—there was no way John was going to get her back down into that cellar.

The butler was still speaking.

"I have often thought that the legend of the banshee must have been born in a drafty house like this one in the wind—it fair whistles and sings some days. I've gotten used to it over the years. I wouldn't let it bother you."

They were back in the front room, looking out over the misty moor. Carole's heart rate was just getting back to normal after their scare, and she was beginning to feel rather foolish at having been spooked twice in the same day.

"So Mr. Blacklaw doesn't use the cellar at all?" John asked.

Carole was only giving the conversation half her attention. She was looking out over the moor, where the mist had lifted enough to see a couple of hundred yards of wet heath and scrub.

"It's not my place to say, sir," the old butler replied to John. "But as I said before, it hasn't been used since your grandfather passed away. It wouldn't have seemed proper."

"I would like to ask you some questions about that night, if I may?" John replied.

"I'll have to ask the Maister if he approves."

"Of course—I don't want to do anything to rock the boat around here."

Carole didn't hear the butler's reply—her attention had been caught by a darker shadow, just within the fog, a hunched figure out on the boggy ground, tramping along with head down—two hundred yards out and heading straight for the house.

"It looks like we're about to get a visitor," Carole said, as the fog rolled in again, obscuring the moor and engulfing the figure in its folds.

"I doubt that very much," McKinnon said, and left them alone, but not before Carole had seen the look in his eyes—he looked just as John had when they'd run up out of the cellar—he looked terrified.

12

After coffee Carole declared that she'd had quite enough excitement for one day and was going to lie down upstairs, but John was too wired to rest. Everything they'd seen and heard so far merely served to confirm that there was indeed a story here that needed to be ferreted out. Maybe McKinnon would have some insight that would enlighten the whole matter—or maybe there was something else in the box of tapes, some tidbit of detail that he could use as a hook into the rest of the story.

He took a cup of coffee through to the library and got the reel-to-reel machine set up with another tape—this one from just a week before the last dated one in the box. Once again his grandfather's voice spoke to him from decades past.

"Blackie is not quite persuaded on the brilliance of my idea, but he has agreed that his cellar would be the ideal spot for filming, and has gotten into the spirit of things by clearing it out and providing some local color with chains, manacles, and whatnot. We did a test sound-check down there earlier, just to make sure the acoustics were going to be right, and the vault does indeed provide an echoing emptiness to voices that will be most appropriate when we come to the ritual itself.

"Mrs. McKinnon, the housekeeper, provided some unintentional hilarity today by declaring me a bad influence on Blacklaw—how little she knows of her new Master. She was also adamant that she would not be staying in the house for the duration of my visit, declaring herself a God-fearing Christian and not about to put up with any works of 'Auld Nick.' If she had not left in such high dudgeon, I might have been tempted to include her in the documentary for some local color. Her husband is a poor substitute in the charisma department, being as dour a Scot as you're ever likely to find, although he already seems devoted to Blacklaw and will brook no nonsense from the younger ladies and gentlemen of our crew.

"We start rehearsals today, and I have already chosen which passages from the book we will use. From now until the final shoot it is simply a matter of organization and choreography. My excitement is growing. We are almost there."

After a brief pause of hissing emptiness, the volume kicked in again. At first John wasn't sure what he was listening to, for it consisted of clangs and rattles, like equipment being set up. Then old Hugh spoke and the situation resolved—it was a recording of a rehearsal, and a particularly chaotic one at that. He heard loud arguments alongside shouted pleas for attention and a great deal of disgruntled moaning, mainly from the female members of the cast who were being forced to hang around in a cold, wet cellar in very little clothing.

Finally Hugh shouted "Action!" and things started to happen, although without vision it was almost impossible to make sense of proceedings. Feet slapped on stone, somebody somewhere groaned in either ecstasy or pain, and, just at the edge of hearing, a camera whirred, recording it all.

After what seemed like an age, singing started, a high-pitched chant that sounded strangely familiar. As the singing rose to a crescendo, Hugh's voice joined in, booming and echoing as if amplified above all the rest. The tape recorder buzzed and throbbed in sympathetic vibration and the temperature in the library seemed to drop alarmingly.

John leaned over and switched the machine off, too quickly, succeeding only in snapping the tape so that the broken ends spun and lashed before finally coming to a stop.

The library fell quiet again, so much so that John jumped with a start when a voice spoke in the doorway.

Old McKinnon stood there, the fear plain in his eyes.

"I haven't heard that since it was recorded," he said softly. "God help me, I should have stopped it. The missus said it would all end in tears, and for once she was right."

"Tell me," John replied. "He was my grandfather—I deserve to know."

The old butler seemed uncertain, then looked at the box of tapes and seemed to come to a decision. "We did something stupid," he said. "We meddled with something that should have been left well alone, God help us all."

"What do you mean?" John asked.

"Come through to the kitchen, sir," the butler said. "The Maister has his domain, and I have mine. I'll be more comfortable speaking through there. "

John saw the old man cast a nervous glance up into the rafters, then back away from the door, as if afraid to enter. He rose and followed McKinnon out into the hallway and through to the rear of the house. They went through a door and into a kitchen that would not feel ashamed in a top restaurant, all stainless-steel butler's sinks and row after row of hanging copper pots and pans.

The old man went straight to a tall wooden cupboard and took out a bottle of Scotch and two glasses.

"I don't usually drink while I'm working, but this a tale that needs a stiffener to tell, if you'll join me?"

John was never one to turn down good liquor. He joined the old man at a long table that was worn and scarred with what might be centuries of use. The butler poured three fingers of Scotch for each of them, and downed half of his in one gulp before speaking.

"The missus is away into Dingwall to do some shopping," he began. "Which is just as well, for neither she nor I have spoken of this for many a year now—although we have been living with it."

John had immediate questions but held his tongue, as the butler clearly needed to get something off his chest.

"We were all much younger then, of course—the missus and I were barely out of our twenties, and we were still new at running the house. We'd heard stories before coming here—everybody for miles around knows about the auld house—but we weren't superstitious folks. Anyway, if you were to believe every story you heard about any auld house in Scotland, you'd think there was a ghost or ghoulie in every one of them. Besides, times were hard and we needed the work, so when the Maister put an advert in the Inverness paper for housekeepers, we were first in line.

"The Maister took to us straight away, and we to him, and those early days were the best ones we had here—the Maister came up from London when he could manage, and the rest of the time we had the place to ourselves. But it all went sour when your grandfather had his stupid idea.

"Moira—that's my wife—told them; she told them both that no good would come of it, and she even went to live with her ma while the filming was going on. But Mr. Fraser would not be swayed—he seemed driven, even obsessed, with his plan.

"I thought it all a bit of harmless fun, back before that last night. I didn't share the missus's apprehension, and I was enjoying the whole thing. Working with the film crew, seeing the Maister and your granddad together like we'd seen them on the telly, even setting up the cameras and lights in the cellar proved to be a bit of a lark all around. And it didn't hurt that the girls they brought up from London were very pleasing to the eye.

"It had all gone smoothly, and I was looking forward to seeing the wife the next day when we got to that last night of filming, but as soon as the chanting started I knew we were about to do something very stupid. I cannot put my finger on it, but something in the atmosphere changed, and suddenly it wasn't such a lark anymore, and if the Maister hadn't needed me, I'd have been much happier almost anywhere else at that moment.

"The girls danced as the cameras rolled, and the old vault echoed and vibrated as if a train was going by overhead. Your grandfather had a big smile on his face as he made his way to the painted circle.

"I believe the Maister had felt the same change in the air that I had, and was of like mind to me. I followed him over to the painted circles and tried to stop Mr. Fraser, but it was no use—he was adamant that the show must go on. He laid down on the floor, shouted out the chant—and all the lights blew at once.

"I was nearest the door and was able to feel my way back upstairs and replace the main fuses. I helped the crew and the girls up the stairs and out into the light, and missed the Maister going back down to the cellar. The first I knew of your granddad's death was when the Maister came back up the steps, his face white and shocked—he looked to have aged ten years in ten minutes. I went past him down into the cellar myself to have a look—and you know by now what was there—Mr. Fraser, just lying there, staring, dead as a doorknob."

McKinnon stopped to pour himself more Scotch, and John thought the story was done, but the butler wasn't quite finished.

"If I had known then what was to come, I'd have taken the missus to her ma's place and stayed there permanently, but God help us, we stayed here, and we've lived with it—for forty-five years we've lived with it."

"Lived with what?"

McKinnon gulped down his Scotch.

"That part of the tale is for the Maister to tell you," the old butler said. "It's not my place. Let me just say that you couldn't pay me enough to go into yon library on my own after dark, and leave it at that, shall we?"

"No—let's not. What's in the library? I need to hear the story."

"And the Maister needs to tell it—he's needed to tell it for many a year now. But you'll have to bide your time—he needs his rest. He'll see you tonight, and may be well enough to tell the tale. But I must go now. The missus will be back any minute and there's chores to attend to, if you'll excuse me?"

Now that his part of the story was told, the old man was back to being all politeness and business, and John found himself getting hustled out of the kitchen and back into the hallway before he could ask any more questions.

A chill breeze followed him upstairs to the bedroom, and John thought it came, not from the cellar, but from the library.

13

Carole woke up at the sound of John opening the bedroom door. She hadn't intended to sleep, merely rest her eyes for a bit, so was surprised to check the clock and see it was already late afternoon. The flowing fog outside the window thickened the gloom and made it feel even later. She was vaguely aware that she'd had a disturbed sleep, strange dreams verging on nightmares, and that they'd involved both mist-covered moorland and dank cellars.

This place is definitely getting to me.

John didn't help matters by bringing her up to speed about his talk with the butler and his intimations of spooky goings-on in the library.

"So you're saying that your granddad's ghost has been hanging around a dusty old library for more than forty years now?"

John nodded. "I'm not sure I believe it—but the folks that live here certainly do."

"We're letting our imaginations run away with us," Carole said. "If this place was in London we'd be laughing all of this nonsense off as preposterous."

"Whether we believe it or not is neither here nor there, is it?" John said. "The people who live here have a story to tell, one that's getting more interesting by the hour. I'm getting close to getting to the heart of it—I can feel it."

"I believe you heard something … Maybe it was in the library itself?"

He lay down on the bed beside her and she nestled against him as he spoke of his hopes—high-profile features in the Sundays, maybe a book deal, and possibly even some television appearances. John was pinning his future on what he was learning in this house. She wasn't sure it was entirely healthy, but he was as excited and focused as she'd seen him in a while, so she'd give him his head—for a while longer at least.

They lay that way in silence for a while before getting up to wash and change for the evening meal.

When Carole emerged from the bathroom, John was listening to his recorder again, playing Blacklaw's interview of that morning. He was going over the section where he said he'd heard something strange, but there was still just Blacklaw's whispering voice, and after hearing the same sentence five times in quick succession, Carole asked him to stop.

"There's nothing there—not now. I believe you heard something—but maybe it wasn't on the tape at all? Maybe it was in the library itself?"

Whatever she'd said, it made an impression. John suddenly got agitated.

"I should have seen it—it's the library—that's where the story is. That's where we'll get to the truth of it."

"That's as may be," she replied. "But if you're not ready in ten minutes, I'm going to eat your supper."

As they went downstairs a quarter of an hour later, she saw John glance towards the library door. She took his hand.

"Later," she said. "The old man is expecting us—let's at least try to be polite."

He didn't argue, although he had a last look before they went through to the front room.

Their host was already in his seat at the top of the table. He looked better than he had that morning, with more color at his cheeks, and less of a tremble in his hands as he lifted a glass to salute them on their approach to the table.

"I hope you made the best of a bad day?" he said. Carole merely smiled—she had a feeling that tales of splashing on the moors and skittering in the cellar were not what the old man had meant.

John was clearly champing at the bit to ask questions, and she had to give him a kick under the table, twice, to curb his enthusiasm, before he went quiet enough to allow their host to control the ebb and flow of the conversation.

At first it was all just small talk—about the desirability of getting, and keeping, good housekeepers, about where their meal had been sourced—venison from the hills, salmon from the rivers, and liquor from the peat-filled waters of both. McKinnon fetched and carried platters of food—again, enough to feed twice their number. Carole found that she was hungry again, and took to it with gusto. Even Blacklaw managed to eat a good half of what was put in front of him. Carole couldn't remember having a better meal.

After the last dish had been taken away, they retired to the library for coffee and more Scotch, and the conversation finally turned once again to John's grandfather.

Blacklaw pointed at the box of tapes.

"Did you listen to the last one?" he asked.

John shook his head. "Not yet," he replied.

"Then please don't," Blacklaw said. "At least not in this room. The consequences would be unpredictable and quite possibly dangerous."

"Tell me," John said. "Tell me what's so special about this room. Your butler hinted at some things, but I need to hear it from you."

"And I cannot persuade you to let the matter lie?"

John shook his head again.

"I'm afraid not. It would gnaw at me forever if I dropped it now, when I'm so close."

Blacklaw sighed. "I had hoped you might be satisfied with the detail of Hugh's death, but I can see you have inherited his stubborn streak along with his looks. Very well then—you shall have another story—or another part of the same story. But first, pour us all a drink if you please. As McKinnon is fond of saying, this one needs a stiffener."

Carole did the pouring duties, and limited herself to a smaller glass than the ones she poured for John and their host. John took out the recorder again, set it running, and Blacklaw began.

"As I've told you, Hugh got a quiet funeral, and we all went on with our lives. I decided to move here permanently, and resolved to live a life of quiet retirement. The library came with the house, lest you're thinking I built it, and I have barely perused a tenth of the contents, but I liked coming in here to sit by the fire of an evening and wallow in history and learning with a book and a drink. It made me feel rather like the lord of the manor, and appealed to my vanity.

"It was sometime in the first winter that my grief faded enough to allow me to listen to these tapes that Hugh had left behind. I remember it was a harsh one, and we were cut off for many days by storms and heavy snow. I sat here on those nights, listening to the wind whistle and howl, and reliving old adventures in warmer climes, laughing and crying along with my old friend.

"And then, one night I finally got to the tape I was dreading—that last one. I almost didn't play it—I even considered burning it, but I'd listened to all of the rest, and felt that I might get a sense of closure by completing the set. I set up the machine and let it play out that final, mad, night.

"Despite the heat of the fire, the library felt quite as cold and dank as the cellar. I heard again the sounds of girls dancing, the high chanting was sent echoing through the library, and I believed I heard an answering echo from the cellar—I don't know if you noticed, but it lies immediately below these chairs. The chanting on the playback rose to a crescendo. In my mind's eye I saw it all again—Hugh walking, smiling, into the circle.

"The playback seemed to increase in volume of its own volition. Several books shook themselves loose from the shelves and fell to the floor with thuds that were like drumbeats in time with the chanting.

"'*Dhumna Ort!*' Hugh shouted.

"The lights in here flickered, the tape ran out and spun off the reel, and everything fell silent. Just as I leaned over to turn off the recorder, something skittered, high up in the rafters.

"That was the first time anyone heard it."

Blacklaw stopped, raised his glass, having to use both hands to stop the shaking, and took a long gulp of Scotch. He looked up toward the roof.

"It has been here with us ever since."

"But what is it?" Carole asked. "Or rather, what do you think it is?"

The old man took some time to reply, and when he did, he had fresh tears coursing down both cheeks.

"I think it is Hugh," he said finally. "Or at least all that's left of him."

14

Blacklaw's announcement brought their evening together to an abrupt end. A minute later he rang for old McKinnon to help him to bed, and left John and Carole in the quiet library.

Both of them looked up at the rafters at the same time.

"If anything so much as moves in here, I'm off," Carole said.

John saw that she was trying to maintain a detached attitude, but wasn't quite pulling it off. Given the day they'd had already, he wasn't feeling all that relaxed himself.

"We should listen to that tape," he said, with more determination than he actually felt.

Carole shook her head.

"Not now. Maybe in the morning, but not tonight. Let's just go to bed."

"It's only ten o' clock."

"Then we'll take the Scotch through to the sitting room. But let's not stay here a minute longer. Please?"

John nodded, and followed her through to the front of the house with the bottle and two glasses. He switched off the lights and closed the door behind him, but he didn't feel any more secure.

Although the two-bar fire in the front room was not switched on, it was still warmer here than in the library, despite the huge bay window looking out over the black moor that, without curtains, must have been a huge heat drain all on its own.

They sat at the table for a while, sipping Scotch and picking at Blacklaw's story.

"I don't quite know what to make of it," John said.

"It's obvious the people here believe it," Carole said.

"Hell—I think I'm coming to believe it myself," John replied. "We've both heard it—there's definitely something in there. And I hesitate to use the word—but I think it's definitely supernatural."

Carole took his free hand.

"We should leave in the morning," she said. "There's nothing else to be learned now anyway."

"Just one more day, sweetheart. I want to listen to some more tapes, and Blacklaw might still have something to tell us. Besides, tomorrow's Sunday. Nothing moves up here on a Sunday."

"Okay," she replied, grudgingly. "But you won't get me back in that library—or the cellar either. If you need me, I'll be in here stuffing my face with cake."

"Good plan," John said.

They both laughed. By the time they finished their drinks and headed to bed much of the tension generated by Blacklaw's announcement had faded into the background.

John couldn't sleep.

His mind kept returning to the vaulted roof of the library and the thing that skittered there.

He remembered his own experience in the dark, with the noise getting closer, and the books thudding at his feet. He'd certainly felt something—a presence of some kind.

Is it possible? Does something of old Hugh survive?

Another thought struck him.

And if there is something still there—is it trying to communicate?

He rolled onto his back and stared at the ceiling. It wasn't as dark as the night before—perhaps the fog had finally lifted outside, for thin watery moonlight came in through the curtains and sent dancing shadows around the room. He watched for a while. Carole breathed heavily and contentedly at his side, and the bed was snug and warm after the damper chill of the main body of the house. But still sleep would not come.

His mind raced—snatches of taped speech, bits of Blacklaw—and McKinnon's—story, images of the high rafters above the books, and the black-and-white photographs from the cellar all jumbled and dancing like a fever dream. Finally he gave in to the inevitable.

He got out of bed, dressed quietly, and padded down, shoeless, to the library in search of answers.

It was after two o'clock in the morning, and he had the run of the house to himself.

The fog had indeed risen and moonlight washed the hallway from the skylight high above. The library was likewise bathed in silvery light from on high, casting black dancing shadows capering around the shelves. He dispelled them by turning on all of the lights and stood there for several seconds until he was sure that the room was quiet and still before making his way to the armchair.

The fire had gone out but there was still some residual heat in the grate. He pulled a chair and the box of tapes over to the fireplace, and set about loading up the last-dated tape in the reel to reel player. On impulse he also set his own recorder going—if there were any noises from inside the library itself, he intended to get a record of them.

Hugh's voice spoke to him again.

"And now we finally come to it. The crew is recording and filming the whole thing of course, but I'd like to have my own little memoir of the occasion too, so I will set it down here—if not for posterity, then for my own satisfaction.

"I had a bugger of a time memorizing the chant from the book, but I think I have it down pat now. If not, if I make a mistake, it scarcely matters, as it is the overall effect we are after—that is what will count in the end.

"All the preparations have been made. We painted the circles on the floor this morning—one of the crew gave me a hand to make sure they accurately matched the diagram. Strangely, as soon as we were done, the cellar felt somehow fuller, and carried the same sense of anticipation as you get in a theatre before a play, as if the room itself is waiting for the final act.

"I will leave this tape running now, for we are about to start. Onward and upward."

The tape went silent for several seconds, then a voice John didn't recognize shouted "Action!" As in the rehearsal he'd listened to previously, he heard the sounds of dancing, feet slapping on stone accompanied by the gradual rise of a high whining chant. It immediately sounded different this time—fuller, with more depth, body and resonance and ringing like a choir in a cathedral. The chant grew louder, more frantic.

The lights in the library flickered, threatened to die, then came on again even brighter than before.

The chant rose to a crescendo and Hugh's voice joined in, shouting out his ritual above the high singing.

The lights dimmed and flared in time to the rhythmic beat. Something beneath John's feet joined in, a pounding like a kettledrum sending vibration up his spine, his chest feeling the beat as if he stood too close to a huge bass speaker.

Hugh's voice rose to almost a scream.

"*Dhumna Ort!*"

The lights blazed, then steadied. A book fell with a thud from the library table onto the floor; then there was only silence.

It took several seconds for John to realize it was over. The tape ran out off the spools and clattered around until he switched the player off.

The house sat quiet around them. Nobody came to investigate any noise, although the pounding John had experienced should by rights have had the house in uproar.

Was it real? Did I imagine it?

He turned off his recorder, stood, and went over to retrieve the fallen book.

It was only when he looked at the spine that he realized that maybe there had been an attempt at communication after all.

He opened the book in his hand. The first interior page had a title he had heard already—it might even be the same one that old Hugh bought in the shop in the Cattlemarket for nineteen shillings and sixpence.

The book that had fallen to the floor was *The Twelve Concordances of the Red Serpent.*

15

Carole woke just after dawn, rolled over and found that John wasn't at her side. His clothes had gone from the chair by the bedside, so she guessed he'd got up early to do some work—it wasn't unusual when he had a story in his sights.

She had a leisurely bath, then opened the curtains to check on the weather before deciding on what clothes to wear for the day. It had been a frosty night. A thin film of white blanketed the moor, and the only fog remaining was over the distant hills or hanging like wispy smoke over the larger of the boggy pools.

Just as she was about to turn away, a movement caught her eye. Someone walked around the corner of the house and into her view, only twenty yards or so away. It was the same hunched figure she had seen from the window—and possibly the same one they'd seen out on the foggy driveway. He was wrapped up in a heavy overcoat that looked several sizes too large. He had a hat pulled down over his eyes casting his face in deep shadow, and he still trudged wearily through the heavy ground, as if his legs were tired and heavy.

She watched him as he crossed her view, heading in the direction of the main door. He went out of sight and she waited for the doorbell to ring. No sound came.

She dressed quickly and went downstairs.

McKinnon was just coming out of the kitchen. He saw her on the stairs and bade her good morning. Apart from him, the hallway was empty, and there was no sign of any new visitors.

She found John in the front room, sitting at the table and poring over an old book. He looked up as she entered. He looked tired and pale from lack of sleep, but was also as excited as a puppy.

"I think Hugh is trying to tell me something," he said.

She had a glance out of the window on the way across the room, half-expecting to see the hunched figure again, but there was only the cold, empty moor.

"Did you see anyone out there this morning?" she asked, but John was oblivious to everything but the book.

"This was definitely Granddad's copy," he said, holding the book in his hands. "He's annotated it with notes in many of the margins. And look..."

He motioned her over to peer over his shoulder. There on the right hand page was a diagram of a naked young man, smiling broadly, stretched out, arms and legs akimbo, on a burning circle.

"I think we know now where the old man got the idea," John said. "And the book is full of occult symbolism—I can see why it drew him in."

He showed her another drawing.

It depicted a figure standing on a border that ran down the middle of the page. On the left-hand side was a winter scene, a snow-covered landscape that twinkled with frost and reflected harsh moonlight in dark shadows that seemed to creep across the view. On the right-hand side it was summer. Children played in a field of green with lambs and foals. A glorious sun lit everything in deep gold. A tall, cloaked figure stood between the two scenes. He had two faces. An old, wrinkled visage watched the summer scene, while a fresh-faced youth watched the snowfall in winter.

Carole couldn't take her eyes off it—it was of the finest quality and had been done by a master of the form. It was also almost certainly worth a small fortune—or would have been had someone not scrawled across it in pen *Not this one*.

Before she could comment on what was probably his grandfather's vandalism, John turned the page, leafing through the book.

"I haven't identified the chant he used yet—but it'll be here somewhere."

She sat beside him. "And what then? What happens when you find it?"

John looked up. "I think he's trying to get through to me. Maybe he has something he needs to say."

"Something he hasn't said to me, the man who was his best friend for decades? Something he hasn't said in more than forty years?" Blacklaw said from the doorway.

John at least had the grace to be embarrassed.

"I didn't mean any offense…" he said.

"And there is none taken," the old man replied, taking his seat at the head of the table. "And please, don't stop perusing the book on my account. It was left here after everyone else had gone, and has sat on the shelves ever since. I'm surprised you were able to find it."

"But I thought I saw someone out on the moor this morning …"

John looked like he was about to say something, then thought better of it. Carole knew that look—he was hiding something from Blacklaw. There was a story there—she'd have to wheedle it out of him later.

McKinnon started to bring in breakfast, and once again Carole found that she was almost ravenously hungry. The three of them made small talk while they ate—there was no mention of the library, or of Blacklaw's revelation of the night before. And all the time John scarcely took his eyes off the book, whereas Carole's own gaze kept being drawn to the window, expecting at any moment to see the hunched figure.

Blacklaw saw her looking.

"Is something the matter?" he asked.

"I feel silly asking," Carole said. "But I thought I saw someone out on the moor this morning—someone I also saw yesterday—and when we first got here."

Blacklaw shook his head. "I don't think so. No one bothers us out here. We're sort of the strange neighbors that nobody likes to meet by accident. Are you sure it wasn't a deer? We get plenty of them poking around."

"It wasn't a deer," Carole replied. "Are there any stories about..." She hesitated, reluctant to bring it up, then ploughed ahead. "Are there any stories of ghosts out on the moor?"

Blacklaw started to laugh, then saw she was serious.

"No," he said. "You need not worry about that. We only have the noise in the library, and that's less trouble than the bats and mice. For an old house, we're remarkably specter-free."

Carole did not feel reassured. Either Blacklaw was wrong, or she was seeing things—and neither of those possibilities caused her any joy.

John hadn't paid attention to any of the conversation. He still had the book open beside his breakfast plate and was scanning it avidly. Carole thought that their host might upbraid him for rudeness, but Blacklaw was an old-school gentleman and maintained eye contact with Carole.

"The McKinnons and I are off to church in half an hour. Would you care to join us? The place is a wee bit on the cold side, but the minister is a marvelous orator, and the singing is lovely."

Carole hadn't been inside a church since her sister's wedding six years before, and was about to turn him down politely, but John still had his head in the book, and the day stretched off for many hours ahead. Maybe some time away from the house was exactly what was needed.

16

Carole had pecked John's cheek, said something about church, and then they were gone. He scarcely noticed that he'd been left alone in the house. The book had him in its grip, as it had his grandfather so many years before. There was a secret here, he was sure of it, but he was as yet no closer to breaking the book's impenetrable code.

He started again at the first illuminated diagram that was on page ten, after nine pages of chemical formulae he wouldn't understand in a hundred years.

The artwork was titled *MALAGMA*, and showed a fiery red serpent coated with thick smooth scales eating the planet, which was depicted as a shining golden disc. The age of the map was evident in the fact that the American continent was not shown, and Asia was mainly India and some of China.

Granddad Hugh had made notes in the margins. His writing was clear and crisp—certainly more intelligible than the text of the book itself.

"This is not part of the process at all; rather, this picture is a symbolic representation of the whole. *Malagma* is Latin, meaning *Amalgamation*. The ultimate goal of this book seems to be a quest, of sorts, a journey that will lead to the amalgamation of the adept's soul, the *microcosm*, with the universe, the *macrocosm* in order to attain oneness with eternity—and effectively, live forever."

John flicked to another page, another illuminated diagram. "*Sublimatio*" was the heading of this one. Hugh's notes informed him that it depicted the transfer of the soul from the *microcosm* into the *macrocosm*, transcending the material world and leaving it behind to soar in the greater cosmos beyond.

The picture showed a shining white dove rising out of a black moorland pool.

John was beginning to wonder whether Hugh had indeed considered the whole ritual thing a bit of a prank—or whether he may have been more serious about attempting some kind of supernatural transformation than anyone had yet imagined.

There was an extra note at the bottom of the same page in Hugh's handwriting that was underlined in heavy pen strokes that seemed to give some credence to John's new theory.

The initiate must prepare to leave the things of his old life behind.

There were more notes—some copious, some only short phrases of agreement or disagreement—studded throughout the two hundred or so pages of dense Latin, old Scots, and complex drawings and word squares. As a work of art it was a beautiful thing, but, to John at least, it was still almost completely incomprehensible. And as yet he hadn't identified the particular passage that Hugh might have used as his ritual.

He took the book and a coffee back through to the library. Perhaps he might have better luck after listening to the ritual again on the tape—maybe that would bring fresh clarity to the words and help him find them in the text.

He sat in the fireside chair and, instead of using the portable reel to reel player decided for simplicity's sake to play back the recording he'd made during the night on his personal recorder. He got an immediate surprise.

There was no extraneous noise on the playback—none of the pounding or high whining chanting that had filled the library, no sound of any skittering or scratching. There was just a flat, almost lifeless replay of what was on the original tape.

Did I really imagine it all? Was it some kind of a stress-related dream?

The only way for John to be sure was to play the original tape again, and he wasn't sure he was ready for that just yet. He sat in the chair with the book in his lap, intending to keep looking for the chant. The pages seemed to swim and melt as he struggled to focus. His eyes felt heavy, the sleepless night finally catching up with him. What with that, the warmth from a freshly stoked fire, and a heavy breakfast channeling blood to his stomach, it was mere minutes before he fell into a deep, dreamless sleep.

17

John should have come with us. He'd have loved this.

Blacklaw had been right about the church being cold, and Carole was glad that she'd taken the time to dress warmly. But he'd also been right about the singing. Voices echoed around the small stone building, filling the place with noise. It reminded her of Sundays in her youth standing in the family row down in Devon while her dad bellowed at the top of his voice and her mum sang in tune, with a high soaring soprano that had always sounded to Carole like the voice of an angel.

Despite her lapsed religion since then, she was glad she'd come with the old man, even after the minister preached a fiery sermon on the sins of the flesh that would have had her blushing in embarrassment in her younger days. The service finished off with a rousing rendition of "Onward Christian Soldiers"—she hadn't sang it since standing in Devon with her parents all those years before, but the words all came back to her in a flood. She found herself putting her heart into it—more like her dad than her mum, making up for her lack of musicality with enthusiasm and volume.

As they left the church she spotted that many of the elderly ladies in the congregation were looking her way, then turning their heads away quickly if she noticed them. Blacklaw saw her looking and laughed softly.

"They think you are my latest conquest," he said. "My reputation as a dirty old man has not yet diminished, it seems."

"Then we had better make sure it stays that way," she replied. She leaned into him, turned her head and planted a full kiss on his lips, before taking his elbow—and McKinnon's place—in helping him down the drive. The elderly ladies of the congregation gave up any pretence and gaped at her openly. She smiled back sweetly, which only seemed to cause them even more consternation.

Now Carole was *really* glad she'd come.

"Thank you," Blacklaw said as they reached the car. "I'll be the talk of the town for weeks now. Just like the old days."

After they got into the back, he turned to her.

"Do you mind if we make a small detour on the way back? There's someone you should meet—it would be a shame for you to come all this way and not see him."

"Not all all," she replied. "You're the boss."

He smiled again.

"If only that were true," he said sadly.

They didn't speak much during the fifteen minutes it took to get to their destination, but Carole hardly noticed—she was completely entranced by the beauty of the countryside they passed through. Light snow had fallen over the higher hills, and frost still covered much of the sweeping slopes of heather and the lower lying peat bogs. The sky had cleared to a cloudless pale blue that felt like living inside an overturned bowl of fine porcelain, and everything looked crisp and newly formed.

McKinnon and his wife—Carole still hadn't spoken a single word to the woman—were up front of the Range Rover, with the butler driving. Carole sat in the back with Blacklaw. As she turned to remark on the view she saw that the old man was plainly getting tired again.

"Please, never mind the detour," she said. "You need your rest."

He waved her away weakly.

"No—this is part of my Sunday ritual, rain or shine, whether I feel up to it or not. I made a promise, and I'll keep it until I'm no longer able. And today is a better day than most for my penance. We are nearly there in any case."

The butler drove them up a gravel driveway to an old—indeed more like ancient—church on the edge of a small forest. It looked like it hadn't been in use for some centuries—hawthorn grew through where a roof had been, and one of the walls had tumbled into a pile of rubble. Ivy ran over the frontage, almost obscuring the remains of what had obviously once been an imposing oak doorway. Carole wondered why the old man had brought her to this place.

As she got out of the car, her breath was taken away by the view. They stood at one end of a narrow loch that stretched, shimmering like silver the whole length, away along a deep-sided valley to a misty horizon. The valley walls were steep, and capped with blue-gray jagged rock and snow-covered peaks, the lower slopes an almost tartan mosaic of soft green, yellow and purple heather. Several hundred yards below their position a herd of red deer grazed as a tall stag kept watch.

It took Carole a minute to take it all in.

"It's beautiful," she finally said. "Thank you for bringing me."

"It is indeed one of the finest views I have seen anywhere

in the world," Blacklaw replied, "But it is not why I brought you. Come and say hello to an old friend of mine."

He took her arm and led her to their right. A small cemetery that looked as old as the church itself sat on the hillside overlooking the view. Most of the stones were aged and beaten so sorely by the weather that the inscriptions could barely be read. But there was one slab of gray marble that seemed almost new, and Carole knew what it must be before they walked around to read who was buried beneath.

"Hugh, say hello to your granddaughter-in-law," Blacklaw said.

The inscription read *Hugh Fraser, 1932–1968, Adventurer, Explorer and Friend. We will meet again.*

"He loved this spot," Blacklaw said. "And as it was to be either here or on the slopes of Kilimanjaro, we—the family and I—decided to keep him close. I come every Sunday, although some days I am barely able to get out of the car—but I come, to tell him what's been happening, although there is rarely much to tell. Today is an exception—today he meets new family."

"And so do I," Carole said. "Thank you."

Mrs. McKinnon was clearing wilted flowers from the foot of the stone and her husband fetched a fresh bouquet from the trunk of the car.

"Would you like to do the honors?" Blacklaw asked.

Carole took the flowers from the butler and knelt by the headstone. The cold immediately gripped at her legs but she hardly felt it as she put the bouquet down.

"I'll look after him," she whispered. "I promise."

She bent forward and kissed the headstone.

Blacklaw laughed.

"Oh, he'd have liked that," he said, and laughed. "He'd

have liked that a lot."

Carole put her hand on the stone to help herself get up, and as she did so had to half-turn towards the old church—just in time to see a hunched figure walk away and go out of sight round the corner.

If she hadn't been with the old man she might have gone after him, but she let Blacklaw take her arm again and lead her to the car. She didn't look back at the view as she got in—somehow its charms had faded as quickly as they had come, and she had a horrible feeling in the pit of her gut that her promise to Hugh might have been a hollow one at best.

18

John woke with a sore back, having been startled from sleep by a sudden sound. It came again just as he sat up in the fireside chair—a skittering, rustling noise from high in the rafters.

Whatever was up there, it was back.

Every instinct told John to get up and run, but he held his ground. He switched on his personal recorder again, hoping for better luck this time, and sat, as still as he could manage, while the skittering noise grew louder, getting closer.

He looked up, but saw only sunlight and a patch of blue sky high above through the skylight. A book moved in its position some twelve feet above his head—not enough to dislodge it from its place in the shelves, but enough to be noticed. The skittering got louder—it reminded John of a cottage in Devon they'd stayed in one autumn, where the mice in the walls had kept them awake most of the night.

Is that all this is—an infestation of vermin?

Another book shifted in position accompanied by more rustling and skittering—ten feet now, and creeping down towards the library floor. Still there was nothing to see, just the skittering sound and the tremble and shake of books that marked its passing.

"Hello?" John said, trying to keep a tremor out of his voice. "Is anyone there? Please tell me what you want me to do."

The photo album fell from the table, the thud as it hit the floor echoing around the room. The skittering got louder still, and the pages of the album rolled over, as if something was flicking through it.

"Hugh? ... Granddad? Is that you?"

The skittering stopped and the library fell quiet. The photo album fell open somewhere near the end, then lay still.

John remembered to breathe.

It was several minutes before he realized that whatever had happened was over—for now. He switched off his recorder before getting up to check on the photograph album. It was open at the second-to-last page, just at the start of the black-and-white photographs of the ritual. The book's fall from the table had moved several of the photos inside the thin plastic sheets within which they were contained. The one on the top left had moved furthest, having shifted half an inch—more than enough to show that there was a second photograph tucked in beneath it.

John slid the newly discovered photo out from beneath the other. It was black-and-white again, and depicted two open pages of *The Twelve Concordances of the Red Serpent*. The right-hand side was a diagram of a serpent emerging from a cave. The left was a long piece of verse, and someone—Hugh again, by the looks of it—had written across the top of it.

"*This is the one.*"

I've found the ritual!

John went straight back to *The Concordances* and flicked through until he found the appropriate page. The lines were in Latin.

Rorate caeli desuper, et nubes pluant iustum.

He took the book and his recorder and went back through to the front room.

He fired up his laptop intent on tracking down the ritual's source. His searches didn't tell him much at first. He found the translation quickly enough.

Drop down dew ye heavens from above, and let the clouds rain upon the Just One.

A search for "The Just One" returned a single short article.

> *St. Brennan's Abbey is long gone, wiped from history, but in the fifteenth century it was the focus of one of the largest religious trials in Scottish history. Twelve monks, long-time residents of the area in the Cheviot Hills of Southern Scotland, were found guilty of heresy. They had renounced Christ and instead had turned to worshipping a being they said lived in the bogs around the Abbey, a being they called the Just One.*

The lights flickered and John's heart jumped into his mouth. But the lights stayed on. He went back to the article.

> *Found guilty, the monks were sentenced to be burned at the stake, but they escaped that fate when a great storm hit. The roof of the Abbey itself fell in. When the storm was over, the monks were nowhere to be found. But local legend says that they can to this day be heard on the moors, singing their prayers to their god. The identity of this god is subject to much conjecture, but …*

John's laptop shut itself down, going black in an instant.

A chant rose, high and loud, from beneath him in the cellar.

Rorate caeli desuper, et nubes pluant iustum.

Peccavimus, et facti sumus tamquam immundus nos, et cecidimus quasi folium universi.

All fell silent once more.

John nearly leapt out of his skin when the front door opened with a loud creak and the others returned from church.

Blacklaw went straight upstairs for a rest, having clearly been greatly tired by his trip. Mrs. McKinnon went back to the kitchen without saying a word, while her husband helped the old man to bed. John brought Carole up to date with his findings as he rebooted the laptop.

"I damned near peed myself," he said, trying to smile. "I know I've always said I don't believe in the supernatural—but what else could this be?" He stopped when he saw how Carole was looking at him. "No—I'm not losing my marbles—at least I don't think so. Let's see if I got any proof."

He switched on his recorder and turned the volume high. And this time he had indeed captured something. The skittering, scratching noise was clearly audible on the tape. John heard himself speak.

"Hello? Is anyone there? Please tell me what you want me to do."

There was more scratching and skittering, then John spoke again. "Hugh? … Granddad? Is that you?"

The tape fell silent.

"That's it," John said, but just as he moved to turn the machine off, he heard it, faint and as if coming from a far distance, but plain as day. A soft Scottish voice he recognized immediately from the tapes spoke.

"Thank you for the flowers."

19

Carole was still staring, dumbfounded, at the machine when McKinnon arrived at the door.

"The Maister will not be down for lunch. Can I get you some sandwiches and beer or would you prefer something hot?"

John had to answer, for Carole was dumbstruck.

"Sandwiches—and plenty of beer—will be fine, thank you."

McKinnon left again, and Carole jumped when John took her hand.

"You heard it too, didn't you?" he asked.

She nodded.

"I don't know what it means, but…"

She interrupted him. "I do," she replied, barely more than a whisper. She sat down hard on one of the dining chairs and fought for calm. Her hands shook as she reached for a glass of water, but after a gulp or two she was able to talk.

She told John about the trip to the grave, and the placing of the bouquet. She left out the part about the hunched figure—matters were weird enough already without adding any more—but John had stopped listening to her in any case.

"I was right," he said. "It is Hugh. And he is trying to communicate."

"I'm not so sure," Carole replied. "What's all this Latin

stuff about? Mad monks and ruined abbeys sounds like something out of a bad seventies horror movie to me."

John shrugged.

"It's that blasted ritual thing again. I think Hugh accidentally found a real magic spell, used it the wrong way, and suffered the consequences."

"Come on, John. There's no such thing as real magic."

He pointed at the recorder.

"And there's no such thing as voices from beyond the grave. But that's exactly what we've got here, and..."

"And what—your granddad died in this house forty-odd years ago and is still here now? Why?"

John shrugged again. "I don't know why—but I mean to find out."

McKinnon arrived with a tray of sandwiches and a pitcher of beer before Carole could formulate a reply.

John ate while surfing the web.

"What are you looking for?" she asked.

"Two things—the ritual itself, and any information I can find on 'The Just One'. There's not much on either as far as I can see. The first part of the ritual is from an old medieval madrigal, that much I do know. As for the thing the monks might have been worshipping—there's very little data. The article I was reading when my laptop crashed calls it 'an earth spirit'—whatever the hell that might be. It's all very vague, I'm afraid."

"Smoke and mirrors, that's what it is. And what will you do with this information if you do find it?" Carole said. "I'm not convinced it's got anything to do with that voice on your tape—that could just be an anomaly, some electromagnetic thing you picked up from the old reel-to-reel player."

Even she didn't believe that one, and John was dismissive.

"What are the chances of an 'anomaly' mentioning flowers and thanking you? Come on, Carole—you know what this must be, don't you?"

She wasn't thinking about monks and chanting—she was thinking about hunched figures trudging through bogs, getting ever closer. It felt like she was being stalked. She took a hefty slug of beer, and the bitterness and tang did much to anchor her in reality.

"I'm just having trouble getting my head around it," she replied. "And I still don't see what good any of this information is going to do you, even if you do find something."

John was quiet for a minute before answering.

"What if I could talk to him?" he said softly. "What if I could talk to Granddad?"

He went back to his laptop and sat scribbling notes. Carole ate more sandwiches than were good for her, her mind racing. She kept coming back to the hunched figure.

Is he the Just One?

She couldn't make herself believe it. A voice from the Great Beyond she could just about handle, but not some kind of ancient spirit worshipped by monks in centuries past—it was just too outlandish.

After a while John closed the laptop.

"Are you done?" she asked.

He nodded.

"I know what I have to do now," he said. He held up a sheet of paper covered in his crabbed handwriting.

"The ritual in the old book is slightly different from the ones I've found online—it's been transcribed wrong somewhere at one end or the other. I believe that's why it rebounded on Granddad and killed him. I wonder if he even knew what he was doing? If he'd done some research he'd have found it was dangerous—but maybe that was the point? Anyway, the experts in this kind of stuff all say the same thing—it's meant to summon the unquiet dead."

"Well, that doesn't sound good," Carole replied, trying, and failing, to get a laugh from John. He had his head down, intently studying the sheet of paper.

"I'm going to do it, Carole," he said softly. "I'm going to talk to Granddad Hugh."

He wasn't to be dissuaded. He got up from the table, ignoring Carole's protestations, and headed for the door.

"Wait!" she shouted. "Just think rationally about this for a minute would you?"

"Rationality has got nothing to do with this, sweetheart," he said from the door. "This is my heart talking, and it knows what it wants."

By the time Carole got to the door, John was already in the library, standing next to the fireplace. He started to read from his notes, a singsong voice that gained in strength and volume as he got into the rhythm of it.

"Rorate caeli desuper, et nubes pluant iustum.

"Peccavimus, et facti sumus tamquam immundus nos, et cecidimus quasi folium universi."

John's voice rang and echoed, filling the room. Something beneath them responded; a pounding like a drumbeat sent vibrations running through Carole's body and set her teeth on edge.

John's chant changed, from Latin to something she didn't recognize but that sounded distinctly Scottish,

"Ri linn dioladh na beatha, Ri linn bruchdadh na falluis, Ri linn iobar na creadha, Ri linn dortadh na fala."

The drumbeat got louder. Dust disturbed by the vibration drifted down from the rafters to fall around them. Voices seemed to rise from below to join in as John continued, a repeat of the previous phrase sung now by a choir, a throng, a myriad of singers in a chorus that rang and bellowed like a huge church organ.

"Ri linn dioladh na beatha, Ri linn bruchdadh na falluis, Ri linn iobar na creadha, Ri linn dortadh na fala."

Carole staggered, almost fell, buffeted by a cold wind that blew through the library like a gale, sending books flying off the shelves to flutter like wounded birds before crashing to the ground and lying still.

The chorus rose to one final cry.

"Dhumna Ort!"

The floor bucked and swayed, and once again Carole almost fell. She stumbled out of the library, into the hall and through into the dining room. She was just in time to see a hunched figure turn and walk away from the big bay window and off round the corner of the house. When she went over to look, a thin film of ice on the glass was already starting to melt.

20

John stood in the suddenly quiet-again library, waiting for a sign. Nothing moved apart from the drifting dust dancing in the afternoon sunbeams.

"What the blazes do you think you are doing?"

Blacklaw, still in his pajamas and wrapped in a dressing gown several sizes too big for him, stood in the library doorway supported by the old butler.

"It didn't work," John said. "There's something I'm not seeing."

Blacklaw shook his head, sadly, his anger suddenly dissipated.

"Do you think I haven't tried, boy?" he said softly. "Come through to the front room. McKinnon will fetch us a drink and you can tell me."

John followed the old man into the sitting room. Carole stood there, eyes wide, shaking like a leaf in the breeze. John went over quickly and took her into a hug.

"It's okay," he said. "It's over. It didn't work."

Carole held him tight, then pushed him away, looking into his eyes.

"Just don't try anything like that again, okay? No more; we're done here."

John wasn't sure of that, not by a long chalk, but she needed to hear something, so he agreed.

"Yes. We're done."

McKinnon arrived on cue with the Scotch.

"Let's have a drink," John said. "I think we both need one."

He saw her glance, twice, at the bay window before she went to a dining chair and sat down. Blacklaw took his usual seat at the end of the table, and John sat as close as he could to Carole, taking her hand. With her free hand she downed a large Scotch in one gulp and motioned for the butler to pour another.

She's even more spooked than I am. Maybe she's right. Maybe we should be done here.

John took a slug of his own Scotch and turned to Blacklaw.

"So you've tried before?"

"Many times," the old man replied. "Especially in the immediate years after Hugh's passing. You have got a far more energetic response that I have ever managed. But the end result is much the same—he never speaks."

John didn't say anything, but switched on his personal recorder and played it back.

"I recorded this earlier—you must have been well on your way back from church by this time."

"*Thank you for the flowers*," Hugh's voice said, and Blacklaw went white as a sheet, all color draining from his face.

"This is some kind of a trick. It must be."

"No trick," John said. "I didn't hear a voice at the time, but it's here on the recording, clear as day."

Blacklaw knocked back his own Scotch and poured another from the bottle McKinnon had left on the table.

"What about this time?" he said softly.

John shook his head. "I didn't set the recorder running. But we should try again," he said, realizing even as he said it that he'd just made a promise to Carole to let things lie.

"No," Carole said loudly at his side. "I don't think that's wise."

"And neither do I," Blacklaw added. "You might not have noticed, but it felt like you nearly brought on an earthquake just now. Let the old boy rest. Please?

John thought it was a strange kind of rest that involved skittering and rustling around an old library for decades, but could see that the other two were resolved in their stance and said nothing.

Blacklaw changed the subject.

"I had another reason for inviting you here," he said. "Beyond telling you of Hugh's final hours, that is. As you can see, I'm getting on a bit, and getting worse every day now. I don't have long left to me—and I have no family of my own to speak of. Hugh was the closest thing I've ever had to a brother—and that's why I'm leaving this house to you when I go."

It had come so suddenly that John didn't know how to reply. He looked the old man in the eye, looking for any sign that it was a joke, but Blacklaw was deadly serious.

"There'll also be some money from the estate—enough to pay for the annual upkeep, I shouldn't wonder. I had a new will made up after you contacted me, so everything is legal and above board. There are two caveats. I want to be buried beside your granddad in the churchyard, overlooking the view. The only other stipulation I have is that the McKinnons are allowed to see out their own lives in this place, which is their home as much as it is mine; but beyond that, it will be yours to do with as you like."

"We can't accept it," Carole said, but Blacklaw waved her away.

"You can, and you will. Look at the pair of you. When you came here on Friday it seemed you were close to ripping each other's throats out. You were tense, moody and irritable—just like every other city dweller I've ever met. Now look at you. Admit it—you're happy. You're relaxed, even despite the experiences, real or imagined, of the weekend."

John had to admit that the old man had a point. He hadn't felt so alive for a long time—and he hadn't even realized he was still holding Carole's hand, and had her head rested on his shoulder.

"This place is good for whatever ails a person," Blacklaw said. "It's worth putting up with the occasional noise in the library from your grandfather. Look—I know it's a lot to take in, and I'm off for another lie-down. I've had more than enough excitement today already. Take some time to think it over—we'll talk again over dinner this evening."

McKinnon had once again divined his master's needs and was standing at the door. He came over to the table, helped the old man to his feet, and they shuffled off together into the hallway and out of sight.

Blacklaw's bombshell had driven all other thought's from John's head. "Well, I didn't expect that," he said.

"We can't take it," Carole replied. "What are we going to do with a place like this?"

"We could move here?" John said, and got a laugh.

"What, you'd give up your trips to the pub? No more curries, no theatre, no cinema—no friends. Oh yes—I can see that happening."

"Perhaps he was right," John said quietly. "Perhaps we do need to think this over."

Carole poured herself another Scotch.

"Maybe we could rent it out—or sell it on," she said. "It's probably worth less than a one-bedroom flat in Mayfair, but it would be something. We'd have to get the cellar floor cleared, though. Any buyer would run a mile at the idea that Satanic rituals had been performed in his basement."

Carole kept talking about possible buyers, but John had stopped listening.

The cellar—I forgot about that. Any ritual has to take place within the prescribed circle—it says so in the book. That's where Granddad died—and that's where I'll be able to talk to him.

21

Carole drank more Scotch than was good for her—mainly to try to rid herself of the feeling that the Hunched Man was somehow focusing its attentions on her in particular, and also to cope with the shock of learning of their forthcoming inheritance. Of course, it might be years away yet—more probably sooner given Blacklaw's obvious ill health—but the thought that John might actually want to move to this place filled her with consuming dread.

When she stood from the table, her legs threatened to give way beneath her, and John had to lend a shoulder for her to lean against.

"I think I need a kip before dinner," she said, slurring her words rather more than she would have liked. The Scotch had obviously won in the battle for her sobriety.

"I think we could both do with a bit less excitement," John replied.

She let him half-lead, half-carry her upstairs. She almost fell into the bedroom, then collapsed, fully clothed on top of the covers.

She was asleep in seconds.

She woke in darkness, having no idea how long she'd slept. Her mouth felt like something small and furry had slept in it and her head pounded with the onset of an instant hangover. She rolled out of bed and staggered to the bathroom. A splash of water on her face made her feel almost human. She turned back to the darkness of the bedroom.

"God. Why do you let me do this to myself?"

It was only when there was no answer that she realized John had left her on her own again. She wasn't surprised—she'd drunk most of the Scotch on her own and had passed out as soon as she'd hit the pillows. He was probably still stoked about his earlier research and experience.

I should never have had so much whiskey.

She stepped into the bedroom then quickly retreated back under the light in the bathroom. Despite the fact that the bedroom had appeared quiet and empty, she had a strong feeling she was not alone.

Shadows shifted in the bedroom and there was a soft thump, as if someone had fallen against a piece of furniture.

"John? Is that you?"

She stepped forward, but not too far, unwilling to leave the lit bathroom for the darkness in the main room. From her position she was looking directly at the tall mirror in the far corner. She saw her own pale face looking back at her—just as a shadow passed between her and the mirror—not enough to block her view completely, but enough to let her know she was not alone. She stepped back, intending to shut herself in the bathroom.

At the same instant someone whispered in her ear, a soft Scottish voice.

"Hurry."

She felt a soft kiss on her cheek, and smelled heather

flowers. A shadow passed in front of the mirror again, then she really was alone.

She stood there in silence for several seconds, listening to her heart pound in her ears. When she calmed she realized she could still hear a drumbeat. It came from somewhere far below, and as she noticed it, John's voice rose in a chant to join in.

Rorate caeli desuper, et nubes pluant iustum.

John was in the cellar—and he had started the ritual.

"You bloody idiot!" she shouted at the top of her voice as she ran out into the hallway. Across the landing, Blacklaw's bedroom door opened and he looked out, bleary-eyes and as pale as any ghost.

"What's going on?"

"It's John," she shouted, heading for the stairs. "He's doing that bloody ritual again—in the cellar."

Then there was no more time for talk.

Peccavimus, et facti sumus tamquam immundus nos, et cecidimus quasi folium universi.

The chant filled the house and something in the cellar responded; a pounding like a drumbeat sent vibrations running through the staircase. She felt it thrum in the banister as she almost threw herself downstairs.

"Stop, John. Please, stop!"

Either he didn't hear, or he chose not to.

John's chant changed to the Scottish section she'd heard before.

Ri linn dioladh na beatha, Ri linn bruchdadh na falluis, Ri linn iobar na creadha, Ri linn dortadh na fala.

The drumbeat got louder as she reached the cellar door. A chill wind blew through the hallway, making it a struggle for her to stay on her feet. Voices rose from below to join in the chorus as John continued, a repeat of the previous phrase sung now by a choir of guttural voices.

Ri linn dioladh na beatha, Ri linn bruchdadh na falluis, Ri linn iobar na creadha, Ri linn dortadh na fala.

She took the stairs down—three, four at a time—and launched herself into the cellar just as the voices rose in one final cry.

Dhumna Ort!

22

John heard Carole call out, but was too caught up in the moment to reply. The decision had been an easy one—he'd watched Carole sleep for a while, but the thought of the cellar and what might wait there for him had consumed him.

Let's get this done.

Once he'd made the decision, it had only been a matter of minutes before he made his way down to the cellar with his sheet of notes. He hadn't hesitated in stepping into the circle, despite a sudden chill that gripped him hard. The chant had poured out of him in one easy, almost breathless, song.

And now he stood in the center of the ritual circle.

Waiting.

The first sign came with the now-instantly recognizable skittering noise in the darkest corner of the room. The neon light overhead flickered then dimmed, thickening the shadows. The skittering took advantage of the extra gloom to move closer, although there was still nothing visible.

"John, come out. Please come out," Carole said, but she sounded far away, inconsequential, and when he looked in her direction it was like looking down the wrong end of a

Only the eyes were remotely human, although they were fully black, all pupil.

telescope to see a figure struggling to make headway, as if battling a strong wind. As he watched, old Blacklaw, still in his pajamas, joined Carole at the foot of the stairs, and the two of them now joined in calling out to him.

Their words were lost in a rising din as a new chorus of deep, guttural chanting accompanied the skittering. A coarse madrigal filled the cellar with a song of longing and pain.

Rorate caeli desuper, et nubes pluant iustum.

A gray shape moved through the shadows, coming closer.

"Hugh? Granddad?" John said.

The skittering increased to frenzied scratching. The gray thing came forward to the edge of the circle—too low to the ground to be anything human, wispy and insubstantial, but thickening with every repeat of the deep chant.

Rorate caeli desuper, et nubes pluant iustum.

A face, wizened and wrinkled, more rodent than man, looked up at John. A bald scabrous head sat on a bulbous body from which sprouted half a dozen hairy, almost insect-like legs. A mass of moist tentacles in a fringe around the thing's neck writhed and squirmed like a nest of snakes. Only the eyes were remotely human, although they were fully black, all pupil. They held John's gaze with a stare that spoke of an insatiable hunger as it scurried over the outer ring and into the circle, coming straight for him.

Carole saw the thing reach John's ankles and start to climb up his body.

"John!" she shouted, but it was as if her voice was lost in a wind, swallowed by the chanting which rang all around them, setting the vaulted cellar ringing like a great bell.

She managed to turn her head to look at Blacklaw, but it was immediately obvious the old man would be no help. His eyelids fluttered, the eyes below rolling in their sockets, and she had to move quickly as he fell towards her. She caught him in her arms, and was about to lay him on the floor when a hunched shadow loomed over them both.

She smelled heather flowers again, and felt the touch of a soft kiss on her cheek.

"Stay here," the soft Scottish voice whispered in her ear. She looked up to see a spectral form loom above them. It was thin and unsubstantial, like thin gauze, but one facet was clear as day.

It had John's face.

The thing climbing up John's torso had no feeling of weight—just a deep cold that ate into John's bones and rendered him immobile, unable to so much as twitch as the guttural chanting rose, and rose again, and the thing—*The Just One*—climbed higher. It reached his chest, his neck. John felt tentacles tickle at his chin, then ice cold lips pressed against his own and started to suck.

A weakness spread fast, as if his whole fiber was pouring out and into the apparition. And as he weakened, so the thing gained weight, grew substantial—grew heavy against his chest, so much so that he was forced to his knees, then all the way to the ground as darkness and cold and a deep, bottomless despair ate at his soul and dragged him away.

Carole still felt like she was wading in thick treacle, but the hunched apparition had no problems. It strode forward, still in that bent-over gait she'd seen out on the moor and in the graveyard. It made straight for the ritual circle.

John was on the ground, something with too many legs and not enough body wrapped around his chest and clamped face to face at his mouth. He wasn't moving, although she saw that the attacking thing's body swelled and deflated—as if it were feeding.

"John!" she cried out again, but her voice was lost among the roar and din of the chanting. She could only watch as the hunched man strode into the ritual circle to go to the aid of his grandson. His form bent and started to tear at the Just One with arms that were too insubstantial to do much damage. The chanting rose to another level, sending dust and earth patterning down from the cellar roof. Blacklaw moved feebly in Carole's arms, looking firstly up at her, then over to the circle. The hunched man chose that moment to look around, giving Carole and Blacklaw a good look at his face.

"Fraser!" Blacklaw shouted. "Hold on. I'm coming."

Like a man half his age, Blacklaw stood and broke into a run.

The chanting faltered as he reached the circle. Without a pause he threw himself down on John, tearing and mauling at the six-legged thing that thrashed and squirmed but could not escape from the attack. It started once again to lose solidity, become almost transparent. The hunched figure—Fraser—joined Blacklaw, their attack getting more frenzied.

The chanting failed and cut off, like a needle lifted from a vinyl record, and all that could be heard was Blacklaw's breath, heavy and panting as he quickly weakened.

"Help me, Fraser," Carole heard him say. "I'm weakening."

The hunched figure's own attack became even more frenzied, and finally started to have more effect, tearing the Just One into thin wisps that were quickly dissipated in the slight breeze that blew through the cellar.

There was one, last, despairing scream, then Carole found she could move freely. The neon strip overhead blazed into brilliance, momentarily blinding her.

When she blinked and ran to the circle it was to find John trying weakly to sit up. Blacklaw lay on his back, dead center in the circle, a smile on his face as his dead eyes stared at the ceiling.

23

John's recuperation was a long one, and he was put under doctor's orders not to travel. They stayed in the house on the moor, and were well looked after by the McKinnons, despite the fact that the housekeepers were clearly grieving for their "Maister."

Two days after Blacklaw's quiet funeral in the old stone church on the loch she found John in the library. The box of reel-to-reel tapes, mostly burned up, was sitting on top of the fire, and he was feeding the flames with pages from *The Twelve Concordances of the Red Serpent.*

"I think I've got it straight in my head now," he said softly as she went to sit beside him. "It was never old Hugh in the library—his ritual all those years ago called up that thing, the Just One, and it has been skittering around in here looking for freedom ever since. And I think it was keeping Hugh out—wandering the moors until such time as an opportunity arose to reverse his mistake—an opportunity I gave him by using that blasted ritual."

"Do you think it's gone?" Carole asked. "Do you think they're all gone?"

John looked up at the rafters, then stared into the flames. "I don't know. But maybe someone should stay here to make sure?"

She took his hand, and together they fed the last pages

of *The Twelve Concordances of the Red Serpent* into the greedy fire.

About the Author

William Meikle is a Scottish writer, now living in Canada, with fifteen novels published in the genre press and over 250 short story credits in thirteen countries. His work has appeared in a number of professional anthologies and magazines. He lives in Newfoundland with whales, bald eagles and icebergs for company.

He has described himself as "A psyche with a deep love of the weird in its most basic forms, and the urge to beat up monsters." More at williammeikle.com

About the Artist

M. WAYNE MILLER is an illustrator for numerous book and magazine publishers as well as several role-playing game publishers. His list of clients includes Dark Renaissance Press, Tor/Forge, Dark Regions Press, Marietta Publishing, LORE Publishing, Thunderstorm Books, Genius Publishing, Journalstone Publishing, Gamewick Games, Dias Ex Machina, Chaosium, and Orson Scott Card's *Intergalactic Medicine Show*. Wayne continues his quest to learn and grow as an artist and illustrator. He lives in Greensboro, NC, with his wife, Carmen, and a very large cat.

Colophon

This book was typeset in Birch, **Plantin**, and **URW Bernini T**, with Type Embellishments as decorative elements.